Infatuated by A Street Legend
By Nikki Rae

Synopsis

Goddess Jenkins and her sister Journey were born and raised in Camden, New Jersey by their father, Rashaad Jenkins. Rashaad just so happened to be one of the biggest retired street legends around. His name still rang bells in the streets and he was feared by most. Despite his past, he didn't want the street life for his daughters. Goddess and Journey set their sights on "respectable" guys. But that didn't totally protect them from danger. They ended up at the wrong place at the wrong time and bullets began to fly. In the middle of the shootout, the sisters have a run in with two brothers, Princeton and Perry Hughes.

Big time kingpins, Princeton and Perry are far from the type of men Rashaad would ever want for his daughters. But what will happen when the two educated women fall for the streetwise brothers? How will Rashaad react to knowing that his precious girls are doing exactly what he fought his entire life to make sure never happened? How much will each sister's life change when she becomes infatuated with a street legend?

CHAPTER 1

Goddess

"How's my two favorite ladies?" my dad asked me and my baby sister Journey, as we sat down at Outback Steak House.

"We're good, daddy. How are you?" I asked.

"I'm doing just great. I'm just chilling and slinging this dick until I found someone worth settling with," he stated. Journey and I was used to my dad talking to us like that. He's been that way since we were younger. My dad never kept anything from us about nothing and I was glad that he didn't. He taught us what real looked like so no one could ever get over on us with the bullshit. My daddy was our world and we were his. Some people felt like our relationship with our father was strange. They said he acted more as our friend then our father; I beg to differ and we didn't care what other people thought of us no how. We sat and enjoyed a meal with our dad which was something that we did every Thursday night after work.

"What about Ms. Melanie? She seemed like nice woman to settle down with," I asked.

"She would be perfect if she knew how to suck dick. She act like she scared and I don't have time for all that shit," he said, causing me and Journey to laugh loudly in the restaurant.

"Dad, you really sick," I told him while still laughing. "Just teach her how to do it. I know damn well you not about to lose a good woman because she can't suck dick," I stated.

"If she was that good of woman, she would know how to give a nigga head the right way. Honestly, I don't even think she likes doing it. She do it for a couple of minutes then stop," my dad Rashaad said seriously which caused me to laugh even harder. After my dad paid the bill, we headed out. I had to run pass the market before I went home.

My name is Goddess Jenkins and I'm 24. My sister Journey and I were born and raised in Camden, New Jersey. So, my way of giving back to my city is working as social worker at Camden high school where I went all four years and graduated top of my class. I love my job with everything in me. It was nothing better than helping children that needed assistance. Not just that, I love helping the parents as well. I had a lot of resources that people didn't even know existed and I was glad to share them with people. My sister, Journey, is my best friend and the only real female that I banged with besides my cousin Latrice. Latrice is my Aunt Diana's daughter; Aunt Diana is my dad's only sister. My dad raised us by himself. He said my mother left us and him to be with some nigga who had fatter pockets than he did and he refused to let her take us but he told us that she didn't even put up a fight for us. According to my dad, he was working as a bouncer in a night club at the time and that wasn't good enough for her. Long story short, my dad ended up becoming a drug dealer and started making a shit load of money within the first couple of months of dealing. He ended up making so much money that he was able to leave the game within ten years damn near a billionaire. Although my dad wasn't in the streets anymore, he is still a big deal. My dad was now the owner of about ten clubs in different states all named Lucky Charms Night Club.

Work was good and the day went by kinda of fast. I was just happy that it was Friday and I could unwind. Journey and Latrice talked me into going over to Philly to some club. I wasn't really the club type, but I went out with them from time to time and always seemed to have fun. When I got home it was a little after 5 pm. I striped out of my work clothes and walked around with just my bra and panties on until I was ready to shower.

Later that night

About 11 pm, Journey, Latrice, and myself walked into the club liked we owned it. All three of us were beautiful with nice bodies, to say the least. I wasn't the type to brag about myself, but I was pretty confident in my looks. Tonight, I kept it simple but cute. I was wearing a jean romper that hugged my curves perfectly. I left a few buttons undone making sure to show a little cleavage with a pair of clear opened toed heels. I wore my hair cut short with honey blonde streaks. The three of us bopped our heads and sang the lyrics to "Poison" by BBD. We made our way to the bar and sat down. A few seconds later, the bartender came over to take our drink order.

"Can I please have a sex on the beach?" I asked while both Journey and Latrice ordered Crown Apple. I wasn't a big drinker but when I did come out, sex on the beach was all I drank. Three drinks later, the three of us were on the dance floor twerking to City Girls. I was definitely feeling nice. I could feel someone starring a hole in my back. I turned around and looked up and I locked eyes with a gorgeous man that looked like he was standing in the VIP, looking down at everyone. I just continued to dance with my girls. An hour later, we headed outside to so we could go home. It was a little after 2 am and I was tired.

As soon as we got outside, the guy that was watching me was standing out front along with few other guys. When he spotted me, he walked over to me and licked his lips before extending his hand out to grab mine.

"You beautiful, ma. I couldn't keep my eyes off of you," he said while kissing the back of my hand. "I'm Princeton, what's your name?"

"Thank you and my name is Goddess," I told him then bit down on my bottom lip, which I didn't mean to do. Princeton just smiled and I instantly got wet just from his smile alone.

Pow Pow! Gunshots rang and everyone began to scream and scatter. I couldn't move, though. I was stuck right in the spot I was standing in until Princeton fell on top of me and everything went black. When I came to, I was lying in a hospital bed, confused to why I was there. I looked up and my dad, Journey, and Latrice was standing in the corner. Journey was crying as my dad consoled her.

"What happen?" I asked then suddenly remembered that there was a shooting outside of the club. I began to panic at the thought of me being the one who got shot.

"Calm down, baby. Some asshole was outside of the club shooting and some guy named Princeton jumped on top of you so you wouldn't get shot. The bullet did grazed your shoulder but you will be fine," my daddy told me.

"You gotta put these tights and t-shirt on, that's all I had in the car. Your romper was saturated with blood," Latrice stated. I looked at her with confusion. *"If I was only grazed, why in hell was my clothes so bloody?"* I thought to myself.

"Why was there so much blood if I only got grazed?" I asked out loud.

"Unfortunately, the guy Princeton that jumped on top of you was shot. The doctor said if he hadn't the second bullet more than likely hit you neck or part of your head," Journey explained. "I thought we were gonna lose you," she cried, causing me to cry. But the only thing I could think about was Princeton getting shot from practically trying to save me.

3 weeks later

Everything was finally getting back to normal. The pain in my shoulder no longer hurted anymore and most importantly, I was back at work. I had plenty of time that I could use seeing as though I never took days off. I didn't tell anyone what happened because I didn't want anyone looking at me all crazy. Journey was really attached to me at the hip since the night at the club, but I'm not surprised. It has always been us two and if the shoe was on the other foot, I'm sure I would have acted the same way over her.

Journey and Latrice were at my house like they didn't have homes of their own. Of course, my dad was tripping but he still let me have my space unlike his daughter and niece. My dad was trying to get word from the street about who was reckless enough to shoot wildly and hit a woman in the process. My dad was big on the no woman, no children rule. He believed the only person that should get hit in a shootout was the target. He also believed that anything else was a coward. I thought about the guy Princeton just about every damn day and just wanted to see him so I can at least thank him. Well, that's what I tried to convince myself to thinking. The truth is I just wanted to see him. See if he looked as good in the daylight while I was sober as he did in the dark when I had a few drinks in me.

While in my office, I was sitting at my desk going through Facebook trying to see if I could find him on there, but I had no luck. A light tap on my office door broke me from my thoughts and when I looked up, my coworker Samantha was standing in the doorway smiling.

"Why are you standing in my door smiling so hard?" I asked.

"You know I always get happy when Aaron sends you flowers," she said referring to my boyfriend.

"Thanks, I'll take them. You really need a damn man so you can smile when you get some flowers instead of when I get some," I told Samantha and she waved me off.

"I have work to do so l gotta go," she replied before walking out of my office. I just shook my head. and grabbed the card that was attached.

"Hello, Ms. Goddess. I can't seem to get you off my mind. You must be something special to make me take a bullet for your sexy ass. I know I must have read that card ten times in the last three minutes. At first, I thought I was tripping when the note first started and can't lie; I was happy as hell that he reached out. I was smiling extra hard when I saw that Princeton left his number on the back of the card.

"Well, I hope that smile you're wearing is because of me?" Aaron asked, breaking me from my thoughts causing me to jump.

"Hey baby," I spoke while sneakily trying to put the card away in my desk. He looked at me with a side-eye for a moment.

"Who sent you flowers?" he asked. I had totally forgot the flowers was sitting there.

"My dad," I quickly lied. I couldn't believe that I was lying to my boyfriend over a guy that I didn't even know.

"Are you ready to go to lunch?"

"Yes, I'm starving," I told him getting up from my desk. We decided to go to Applebee's to grab lunch. As soon as we arrived and got seated the waitress took our order.

Aaron and I have been together for a little over a year now. My family loves him and the way he treated me. Aaron has never even raised his voice at me, he always treated me with care and respect. The fact that he was sexy as hell was even more of a turn on. Aaron was brown-skinned with a baldhead and a nice full, neatly trimmed beard. We met at a gas station over Philly when I went to pump my gas. He came over to pump it for me and I was glad because I wasn't about that life at all. At that time, we exchanged numbers and we've been together ever since.

"I have a business trip coming up this weekend and wanted to you to come with me if you don't have any plans," Aaron stated breaking me from my thoughts.

"Now you know I'm always down for any kind of getaway, but where is it located at so I know how and what to pack?" I told him.

"We're going to DC," he replied.

"That sounds good, I can't wait." After we ate, Aaron dropped me back off at work. He walked around to the passenger side and opened the door for me to get out. After sharing a passionate kiss, I walked back into work. As soon as I got to my desk, I opened my drawer and pulled out the card that Princeton sent with the flowers and read once more. My phone buzzed indicating that I had a text.

My Boo: I can't' wait to taste that pussy tonight.

Me: I can't wait to ride your face then feel you inside off my tight walls.

My Boo: You're so damn nasty but I love every bit of it. Let me get back to work.

I didn't bother to respond. Instead, I stored Princeton's number in my phone then sent him a text message.

Me: Hello Princeton. I love the flowers but it seems like I should have been the one sending you flowers being as tho you took a bullet for me.

Princeton: That was just one of the many things I plan to do for you, Ms. Goddess.

For some reason, I reread that text twice and still didn't know what I wanted to say. He sounded like he was planning to be around for a while. As I was about to reply it dawned on me that he had sent me flowers and I wondered how the hell he knew where I worked at.

Princeton: Hello? Are you there?

Me: Yes, I'm here. I'm at work. I have a family coming in. May I text you when I get off?

Princeton: You can call or text me anytime you want. I'll be waiting for you. Have a good day.

Me: Thanks and you do the same. Again, thanks for the flowers.

The workday was finally over and it was finally time to head home. I knew I had to cook because Aaron was coming over after work and I wanted to feed him before being blessed with a great sex session. On my way home, I decided to call Journey to see what she was up to.

Friday Evening

Aaron and I just checked into the Four Seasons Hotel when I walked into the Presidential Suite. It was just breathtaking as usual. I loved traveling with Aaron because we always stayed at nothing but the best hotels and had the best times. Aaron was the CEO of this big financial company. He had a meeting in a couple of hours so I knew I would probably go out and do a little shopping. Tomorrow night was the business dinner so I would be able to attend so I had to make sure I turned heads when I walked in. Before Aaron left for his meeting, he left me his card to go buy a dress for tomorrow night. I went to this boutique that I had Googled and they seemed to have nice things. An hour later, I had the perfect dress and shoes. I was sure I was gonna turn a couple of heads and make a couple of women jealous. When I got back to the room, I pulled my from my phone from bag and saw I had a text message.

Princeton: Good evening, Goddess. I was hoping to have heard from you by now. I don't know what it is about you, ma but you been on a nigga's mind ever since the moment I laid eyes on you. I'm out of town right now but when I get back, I would like to see.

ME: Hello Princeton. I'm sorry I've been pretty busy, but I would like to see you as well.

Princeton: It's cool, I understand. As soon as I get back in Jersey, I'll hit you up. Have a nice night.

Me: Goodnight, Princeton.

I couldn't believe I told this man that I would see him when he got back. I was tripping and I really needed to get my shit together before I write a check I can't cash. I needed to talk to someone so I called my sister.

Ring, ring

"Hey Goddess, wassup?"

"Girl, why the guy that took a bullet for me sent me some flowers a few days ago and now he wants to see me and my dumb ass agreed," I told her.

"Look, Goddess, the man did possibly save your life so I don't see anything wrong with meeting up with him and thanking him in person but after that, you need to let him know that you really appreciate what he's done for you. But you have a man and can't see him again," she told me making it sound easier than what it was. It only sounded easy because I haven't shared with her how I think about Princeton every day and that he makes me feel warm and fuzzy inside.

"Yeah, you're right. Anyways, enough about him. What you getting into this weekend?"

"Not much. Me and Trice supposed to go to the mall and do some shopping and she was talking about this comedy show happening in AC tomorrow night, so we might do that," she told me.

"Y'all bitches would wait until I come down here to go to a comedy show," I stated while rolling my eyes.

"Bitch, it ain't our fault that you went and got yourself a corporate nigga and y'all asses gotta chill with a bunch of snooty white folk," she said making me laugh. I talked with my sister for a little longer before hanging up.

I showered and got dressed since Aaron told me to be ready by 7 pm. I wasn't sure we were going, but I did know that it involved eating. I decided to go with a gold sequin one shoulder dress. Just as I was finishing up with my hair, Aaron walked into the room calling my name. When I stepped out, he looked like he wanted to eat me but just licked his lips.

"Damn babe. You looking sexy as fuck right about now. You know I can't leave out of here without tasting you right?" Aaron always had me blushing. That's the one thing I could say. Aaron put a smile on my face all day every.

He picked me up and walked me over to the bed and gently laid me down. He hiked up my dress and slid my panties to the side and started feasting on my sweet spot as if it was his last meal.

"Ahh," I moaned as he feasted on me. He slid two fingers into me and moved them slowly in a circular motion hitting my spot causing me to cum hard instantly. "Oh shit, Aaron! I'm cumming!" I yelled loudly as my body began to convulse. Once I was finished cumming, Aaron got up and went into the bathroom and came out with a rag to wash me off. After placing a kiss on my lips, we headed out the door for our date.

CHAPTER 2

Princeton

Saturday night

Tonight, me and my brother Perry were out of town on some business but all I could think about was shorty from the club. She was bad as fuck and I needed her in my life. That night at the club, when I heard the shots, my first reaction was to jump in front her even though I didn't even know her. I shocked the shit out of myself with that one. I ended up being shot in the shoulder but I was pretty good now. My brother and I were heavy in the streets but we had to be smart about it. We made sure we cleaned our money right. Besides, some of our biggest buyers are some very rich and powerful people that you could ever imagine would be in the drug game. This was some suit and tie fancy shit. After throwing on my custom made all-black Armani suit with maroon burgundy shirt and bow tie, I slipped on my burgundy Stacy Adams shoes. I looked in the mirror and smiled to myself as I ran my hand down my beard. I wasn't cocky by no means but I was confident. I didn't need anyone to tell me that I was a good looking brother. Besides looks, I had the charm and money to go with it. I headed out the door to meet Perry in the lobby. No homo shit but my brother looked just as good as I did. The only difference was, Perry was on the lighter side and I was mocha brown.

We entered the room and immediately became the center of attention and we ate that shit up every time. We were both smiling hard as hell showing all thirty-two's.

"Good evening Princeton and Perry. Y'all looking dapper as usual," the wife of one of our buyers said.

"Well, thank you. As long as your husband stay loyal, we will continue to look dapper," I replied before walking off. I went over and shook a few hands but stopped dead in my tracks when I laid eyes on Goddess and fuck looking like a snack. She was looking like an entire Thanksgiving meal plus dessert. I wondered what the hell was she doing here and who the hell was she with but at this point I didn't care. I've been dying to see her, so I was going over there. "Yo', that's baby girl from the club," I told Perry then headed her way.

"Yo', what you doing? She over there with a whole nigga can't this shit wait?" he asked. "If we were anywhere else, you know I would be down for it, but I don't wanna start no shit in here tonight."

"Nah, fuck all that. I'm going over there," I told him. The sight of seeing her with another nigga was making me sick to my stomach. I knew I was being petty, but I wanted what I wanted and she's what I want. She was smiling and hugged up with the guy that I would assume was her man being as though they were super friendly with one another.

"Hello Goddess, you're looking heavenly right now, how's the shoulder?" I asked as I watched all the color from her face drain and the dude looked like he was turning red. I didn't care that I was making this uncomfortable. She swallowed the lump in her throat before speaking back.

"Hey Princeton, how are you?" she stuttered. The dude she was with cleared his throat. "Baby, this Princeton, and Princeton, this is my boyfriend Aaron. Princeton is the guy that stopped me from being shot." Her dude just mean mugged the fuck out of me but spoke anyway. Honestly, I was just as uninterested in his ass as he was in mine. The thing was, he was about to be irrelevant and yesterday's news because Goddess was about to be mine.

"Well, it was nice seeing you again, Goddess? The two of you try to enjoy the rest the night." Me and Perry walked off and snickered.

"Yo', you wild as fuck for that, bro," Perry said causing me to laugh.

"You ain't seen shit yet," I told him honestly.

I mingled a bit but the only person I could think about was Goddess. She was wearing a gold one shoulder sequin dress with a brush train and a high split. That shit was sexy as hell and I needed to have her right now. I pulled one of the buyers wife to the side so I could talk to her.

"Listen, don't look now but in ten minutes, I want you to go get that woman that's wearing the gold sequin dress away from that man. You can look now," I told her. She slightly turned her head but didn't look too obvious. She gave me a head nod to let me know she knew who I was talking about. "Once you have her, make small talk then ask her to walk you to the ladies room and I'll handle the rest. And if anyone asks for her, the last time you saw her, she was mingling with the other ladies." She just gave me a devilish grin and sashayed across the floor. I walked over to where Perry was standing.

"Yo', I'm about to go holla at shorty in the bathroom for a minute. Just keep a lookout for that corny ass nigga," I told him.

"Nigga, what the fuck? You wild for this one. Homegirl got you tripping," he said shaking his head. I just smiled at him with a devilish smile then walked off.

When I walked into the bathroom, I was glad that no one else was in here because I would have kicked their asses out. Three minutes later, Goddess appeared into the bathroom with the lady I sent to go get her. They were talking and smiling about some bullshit ass conversation that I quickly interrupted.

"I'll take it from here," I told the lady before passing her five hundred dollars for getting her to me as I directed. Goddess was standing there looking shocked and confused as to what was going. I escorted the lady to the door before locking it. "No need to look scared, ma. I needed to get you alone," I told her.

"Are you crazy? My boyfriend is out there," she spat.

14

"Fuck him. He won't be your man for much longer. I'm gonna make you mine at any cost," I stated honestly and cockily. Goddess stared at me like she was about to say something, but I leaned over and kissed her lips. I was amazed at how soft they were. She started to pull away from my embrace but I pulled her back in. "Don't fight this, ma because I know you feel the same way I do," I told her kissing her once more. This time, Goddess didn't fight it but moaned into my mouth and I lost it.

I slid my hands up her dress and she smacked my hand away. "Princeton, there is no way I'm fucking you in this bathroom or at all for that matter," she stated with a shaky voice.

"I know we not fucking tonight I'm about to eat your pussy and you're going to let me and you're gonna enjoy it." I picked her up and placed her on top of the small countertop and slid her panties off. I swear Goddess had the prettiest pussy I've ever laid my eyes on. I wasted no time feasting on her sweet peach. She was trying to run from this tongue lashing but I grabbed her tighter so she couldn't move.

"Ahh God, Princeton! I'm about to cum!" Goddess yelled making dick brick up. She tasted so fucking good. I was whipped already and I haven't even felt what the pussy was like yet. I got up from my knees and just stared for a moment.

"Damn, you taste good," I told her while licking my lips.

"I gotta go, I can't believe I just did that," she said jumping off the little counter. Goddess searched for her panties and then headed for a stall. "Please don't still be in here when I come out," she yelled through the stall. Her little attitude wasn't doing anything but turning a nigga on. I turned the water on and rinsed my mouth out before heading out the door. On the way, out an older woman was on her way in. She looked at me with her nose turnt up and I just smiled.

I knew I had to let Goddess process what had just took place. She was probably pissed that I put her in the predicament, but I bet she'll never forget it and she'll get over it sooner than later. When I walked back into the room, I spotted Perry sitting at the table with Greg but we call him Gee.

"What's up, Gee?" I spoke as I took a seat the table.

"What's up Princeton? It's nice of you to join us. I was wondering where you were at," he replied.

"I had something more important to attend to," I told him. I looked around the room and watched as Goddess strutted in looking around probably looking for that nigga. Our eyes met and her face seemed to soften. I just smiled at her and got back to my conversation. I knew I wasn't gonna be able to stay at this dinner much longer because I couldn't bear to see her with that nigga. "Yo', I'll holla at y'all later. I'm going to my room," I told them before getting up and walked off. I couldn't believe how this chick had me acting. I was way out of character over her and it was driving me crazy. I didn't know what the hell I was getting myself into when it comes to her.

I do know that chicks flock to me and my brother being as though we were the biggest fucking kingpins in Camden, New Jersey where we were born and raised. The Hughes name rung bells and at the age of twenty-seven, we had more money than we could ever imagine. I supply the entire fucking state of New Jersey. Not to mention, I'm a ruthless killer and if fucked with, get fucked over. I didn't take no kind of disrespect of any kind from anybody. The only people that were safe from my hands were women and kids. But if a bitch got out of line, too bad. I had somebody for her ass. I was born and raised into the game. My dad literally started teaching us everything we needed to know. I was five years old and we were going to the gun range at ten. My brother and I was right under my dad in the game so when he was killed, him and I became the head niggas in charge. Perry and I ran shit together. We were equal in the game and I wouldn't have it any other way. My brother was not only my brother; he was also my best friend. I didn't fuck with niggas let alone trust anyone outside of my brother. It was us against the world. Neither of us has girlfriends or kids and didn't plan on it anytime soon.

Don't get it wrong, we had bitches that we fucked around with but we knew they only fucked with us because we were made of money. I wasn't bothered by that at all because I was only fucking with them for what they could do for me. They either had good pussy or good throat; nothing more and nothing less. My mother was the only leading lady in my life. After my father was killed, she moved to California with her sisters and I was actually happy because if anything was to ever happen to my momma because of the life we live, I'll never be able to live.

Goddess was on my brain something heavy. I couldn't figure out what the hell it was about her. I didn't know the first thing about Goddess but everything about her told me she was supposed to be mine. After eating her pussy in the bathroom, I was really hooked and seeing her with that guy had me ready to lose my mind. I couldn't even stay for the rest of the dinner. When I got to my room, I poured myself a shot of 1738 Remy and lit a blunt. I walked onto the balcony and sat down enjoying the air. After I took about three pulls off my blunt, my mind began to ease a little bit. Baby girl had me tripping. I heard a knock on my door and knew it was my brother. I got up to answer and as soon as he walked in, Perry looked at me with a puzzled look on his face.

"Yo', bro, what the fuck is going on with you, man? You know we were supposed to talk a little business with this guy and you just walked off. Since when do we not discuss money?" Perry asked.

I took another pull from my blunt then passed it to him. I slowly blew the smoke out before responding. "I can't even lie, bro, I don't know what the fuck has gotten into me. All I know is baby girl got me fucked up in the head and starting to get pissed with myself for having feelings for chick I don't even know. This shit is crazy," I told him running my hands down my face.

"Hell yeah. First, you jumped in front of a bullet for her then you go over there and disrespect her nigga like what the fuck, Princeton? And what the hell happened in the bathroom?" he quizzed.

"I just ate her pussy and that was it," I replied honestly. He just looked at me and shook his head. I didn't blame him because I knew I was tripping, but I knew until I had her, this shit was probably gonna get worse. Once Perry left, I climbed into bed and grabbed my cell. When I looked down, my eyes grew wide when I saw that I had a text from Goddess.

Goddess: I really don't appreciate what you did tonight. That shit could have caused a lot of trouble. I appreciate you taking a bullet for me, but I really think that we should stop all communication after this text. I will be blocking your number as soon as I send this text so there's no need to respond.

My feelings were crushed after reading her text, I read Goddess's text about three more times before tossing my phone on the nightstand and closing my eyes.

Sunday morning

Me and Perry just got back home and had to go straight to the warehouse. No sooner than we landed, I got a call telling me one of my buyers was fifty grand short and that was absolutely a big problem. I didn't play about my money. I pulled up to the warehouse and as soon as I walked in, I pulled out my pistol and aimed it at Roger. "Where the fuck is money?" I barked.

"I don't know! It was supposed to all be there. I don't know what happened," that pussy cried.

"Neither do I," I told him before put a bullet right through his skull. "Clean this shit up!" I ordered. "I want his boss dead by tomorrow morning," I demanded before walking out. I was tired and need to get some sleep. As soon as I got in the house, I smoked a blunt before taking my ass to bed.

Goddess

Monday morning

As I got dressed for work, I couldn't stop thinking about the crazy shit that happened over the weekend with Princeton. That shit was crazy. Of course, Aaron and I argued over Princeton for the rest of the night. He felt like he was being highly disrespectful and I just sat there and allowed it. That shit that Princeton pulled in the bathroom had me confused. I was pissed but intrigued at the same time. After I texted him that night, I blocked his number so I wouldn't have to read his response. After I was dressed, I headed out the door. I had to be on time because I had a family coming in at 9 a.m. and it was already 8:30. As soon as I sat at my desk, I powered on my laptop and as usual, Samantha appeared in my office as she did every morning.

"Hey girl, how was your weekend?" she asked, smiling brightly. I thought about her question and wished I could tell her the truth but decided against it.

"Girl, it was pretty cool and the food was good," I told her leaving out the fact that I got my pussy ate in the bathroom by the nigga that took a bullet for me while my boyfriend was in the other room.

"That's good. Anyway, my weekend was dry as usual. My sister and her kids came over for a few but that's about all. I think your family just got here," Samantha told me.

A couple minutes later, my family came in needing assistance with their PSEG bill. The lights were in jeopardy of being turned off and they had no way to come up with the money. Even with my resources, it wouldn't be enough to cover their bill. I didn't know what else to do to help until a brilliant idea hit me.

"Miss Smith, I'm not supposed to do this, but I would hate to see y'all in the dark, so if you would allow me to, I would like to pay the bill for you. This is a one-time thing and it has to stay between us," I told her. She looked up at me like she had heard me wrong.

"You would do that for me and are you talking about paying the entire five thousand?" she asked shockingly.

"Yes, I would love to help you," I replied.

"Oh my God! I can't believe you would do this for me," Miss Smith stated as a single tear escaped her eyes.

"It's no big deal. There's no need to cry," I assured her.

"Thank you so much. You have no idea how much I appreciate this and don't worry, I won't tell a sole," she stated. Miss Smith got up and gave me hug. After getting her account number, I walked her to the door then went back to my desk. My office phone rang and I picked up.

"Ms. Jenkins, you have someone here to see you," the receptionist informed me. I wondered who it could be being as though my next appointment wasn't for another hour.

"Send them in," I told her. When my office door opened, my heart damned near jumped out of my chest when I stared into the eyes of Princeton.

"Good morning, Goddess."

"Good morning, Princeton. What the hell are you doing here at my job?"

"I had to see you. Look, Goddess, I don't know how to explain this shit but it's something about you that I just can't shake. I feel like we're meant to be and I know you feel the same way that I do so please don't fight this shit. I will stop at nothing until I have you as mine and I mean that shit Goddess.

"Look Princeton, I can't deny that I do have some weird-ass feelings for you, but I do have a boyfriend so this can't happen," I told him.

"Yeah, but I don't think you understand, you're gonna be mine. And just for the record, I don't give a damn a about that nigga. All I care about is getting to know you and making you mine," Princeton stated cockily. I hated how he made me feel. I knew deep down that I wouldn't be able to resist him but for so long. But I needed to figure something out and quick. I couldn't let him think he had it like that when it came to me so I needed to be strong.

"As I stated before, I have a boyfriend, Princeton and you're going to have to accept that." He laughed and that shit pissed me off. Princeton walked over and got into my personal space and my heart started racing, it felt like it was about to pop out of my chest. Just before he went to speak there was a knock at the door and all I could say was saved by the bell, or so I thought.

"Hey, baby…" Aaron's voice trailed off when he saw how close Princeton and I were standing.

"What the fuck is he doing here, Goddess?" Aaron yelled. I couldn't help but to stumble over my words when I went to talk.

"Baby, he just came to apologize for his actions on Saturday," I lied. I prayed like hell that Use his name here would agree but from the sly smirk, he was wearing told me he wasn't.

"Yeah I just wanted say sorry," was all he said with a chuckle. Later Goddess, he said over his shoulder before walking out the door.

"How long have you been fucking that nigga, Goddess?" Aaron yelled.

"Aaron, I'm not fucking him, but I think we should talk about this at my place before I get fired." Aaron never responded, he just left out the office. When I got to the front desk, he wasn't out there. I told them that I was leaving for the remainder of the day and I'll see them tomorrow. As soon as I got in the house, I called Aaron's phone but he didn't answer. Two minutes later, he was walking through the door.

"Who is that nigga, Goddess because your story isn't making any fucking sense right now," Aaron quizzed me.

"I told you everything, Aaron!" I cried.

"So, why the fuck do this nigga keep popping up?"

"I don't know! I swear!"

"You must really think I'm stupid, Goddess. I think we need to take a break from one another. I always said I was never gonna fight over a bitch that supposed to belong to me. That man is not going to act like that and pop up every damn where if you not giving him no play. So even if you're not fucking him yet, you're damn sure entertaining it," Aaron stated before walking out the house. I called after him but he kept going.

All I could do was cry. Just a few weeks ago, him and I were perfectly fine and now I had a feeling that we were really over. I knew that I fucked up pretty bad. This was all my fault; I was entertaining Princeton I thought about him every day almost all day. I eventually cried myself to sleep.

Later that night

When I woke up, I realized that I had slept for damn near three hours. After using the bathroom I called my sister because I really needed to talk to someone about this.

"Hey Goddess, wassup with you?"

"I need you to come over to talk. I fucked up," I told her.

"I be right there," Journey told me before disconnecting the call. I didn't feel like cooking so I ordered some Chinese food. Twenty minutes later, my sister was at my door. She didn't bother to knock, she just used her key. Journey wasted no time getting to the point.

"Aight bitch, what did you do that you got me here on a Monday night?"

"For starters, I ran into Princeton at the business dinner on Saturday and he walked over and made his presence known totally ignoring the fact that Aaron was standing right there. But to make matters worse, I let him eat my pussy in the bathroom," I told her shamefully. Journey looked at me like I had three heads.

"Bitch, I know you lying right now. What the hell you mean you let that nigga get you in the bathroom?"

"I know, Journey. This shit is crazy. You know I would have never done no stupid shit like that. Princeton really got me tripping. But let me finish the story. He popped up at the job talking about he not gonna stop at nothing until he has me. Of course, with my luck, Aaron pops up at my job and they got into it and Aaron pretty much told me that we should take a break cause he not fighting over something that supposed to be his."

"Damn bitch, you got some Love and Hip-Hop bullshit going on. So what are you going to do? I mean, I know you love Aaron but this Princeton dude got you tripping," she asked me.

"Bitch, tell me about it. I honestly don't know what I'm going to do this shit is crazy. I'm just gonna take some time for myself for now. Aaron wants to take a break so I'm going to fall back," I told her honestly. I didn't know what I had I going in my life right now but this was all new for me. I heard the doorbell and figured it was the food.

"Are you expecting somebody?"

"Yeah, the Chinese man," I told her and we both laughed. After paying for the food, my sister and I went in on that food while we talked about my foolishness.

"Goddess, why the fuck was Princeton at a business dinner? What kinda work he do?" Journey quizzed. The crazy part was I didn't know that answer and never even thought about it until she brought it up. That's how I knew I was bugging for real because I would have normally been all over that.

"I have no idea, I don't know. I didn't even bother to ask. I guess I was so busy focusing on other shit to even wonder why he was there in the first place. Girl, I feel so dumb. I'm tripping over a nigga that I don't know the first thing about."

"Yes bitch, you definitely tripping, but I wanna know what that mouth can do? How was it, bitch?"

"Bitch, that shit was the best and the crazy part is, it was good and I know it wasn't even his best. So, I know I would be turnt the fuck out if the nigga laid me down and feasted on my shit and I didn't have to worry about if I'm gonna get caught or not," I told her honestly.

"Damn sis, he doing it like that? I ain't even gonna lie, that nigga is fine as shit not to mention sexy with mad drip. The fact that he took a bullet for you makes him even more appealing," Journey, said licking her lips.

"Bitch, don't lick your lips when you talking about my man," I told her playfully but was serious as hell at the same time.

"Your man, huh? And bitch, I don't want no nigga that done ate my sister's box. Now if that nigga has a brother or a cousin that can eat good box, then maybe," she said, making both of us laugh. After Journey left, I took a shower and hopped into bed.

Thursday night

The week has been crazy ever since Monday. Aaron refuses to talk to me and Princeton has been blowing up my phone like some kind of stalker, but I refuse to talk to him. I had unblocked him so I could see if he would call or text me after what went down. I really needed to clear my head and figure some shit. I pulled up at Olive Garden ten minutes later than I attended to. When I walked, in my dad and Journey was already seated so I walked over to the table and they had already ordered my drink.

"Hey, dad!" I spoke excitedly as I gave him a tight hug. "Hey Journey," I spoke to my sister before sliding in the both.

"Hey, Princess. Wassup with you, baby girl?"

"Nothing much just chilling," I answered. After we ordered and finished dinner, my dad picked up his drink and took a sip before looking up at me.

"Goddess, how's Aaron?" Before I could answer, Journey, put a sneakily smirk on her face. I knew she was about to start some shit.

"Yeah, how is Aaron doing, Goddess? Oh wait, you haven't talked to him since the day he broke up with you because he caught you with the nigga that took a bullet for then ate your box in the bathroom, have you?" My dad spit his drink out then looked between the two of us as I rolled my eyes hard at my sister.

"What the hell is she talking about? Goddess, I know damn well you're not fucking with Princeton?" I just put my head down pissed that my sister would put me on the spot like that.

"Of course not. I mean, we had a small encounter, but we didn't have sex."

"Well, what exactly did y'all do since it wasn't sex?" he quizzed, taking another sip from his drink.

"He gave me oral sex," I mumbled.

"So, you letting strangers eat your pussy in the bathrooms now, huh? Well, I want you and that nigga at my house at 6 pm sharp," my dad stated firmly.

"Dad, meeting him isn't necessary because nothing is going on the with the two of us. I haven't even spoken to him since last week."

"Look, Goddess, this isn't up for discussion. You must like his ass if you let the nigga eat your pussy in a bathroom while you had a man. It's either that or your ass done turned into a little hoe. So, like I said, I'll see y'all hot asses at 6 pm tomorrow evening." I just sat there and shook my head. When I looked over at Journey, she was wearing a dumb ass smirk on her face. I swore I was gonna pay her back for that shit she pulled.

"Aight daddy, I'll see if he's willing to come over," I told him.

"Nah, you not gonna try, you're gonna bring his ass to me or I'm going to find him. Now, I hate to end this little chat, but I got myself a little playdate in about an hour. I love y'all. Text me when y'all make it home," he told us, kissing both of us on the cheek before leaving the money for the bill. As soon as my dad walked off, I had a few choice words for my sister.

"Bitch, why the fuck would you tell daddy some shit like that?"

"You already know how I do. Let that man meet his soon to be son-in-law."

"Bitch, you play way too much but don't worry, I got something for that ass. And that's not his damn son-in-law. I can't believe this shit. Anyway, bitch, text me when you get home. I gotta go call this nigga," I huffed as I exited the booth. Journey just laughed at my ass. I swear I couldn't stand her at times. When I got in the house, I contemplated if I should call or text. I decided to text to at least break the ice

Me: Hey Princeton. It's Goddess.

Princeton: Wassup? I was wondering when you were gonna reach out to a nigga. I've been texting and calling you for over a week. I was trying to give you your space, but I was about to do a pop-up.

Me: I don't need you doing no more pop-ups. You have stirred up enough drama in my life. But listen, I'm just going to get the point on why I texted you. My father wants to meet you tomorrow night. He wants you and I to come over tomorrow at 6 pm. I know it sounds crazy but honestly, it's not really a request; it's a demand.

Princeton: Well, first and foremost, don't nobody demand me to do shit. But I will go and see what your old man wants but he better not be on no bullshit because I ain't beat. Text me your address so I can pick you up. I'll be there around 5:30 pm so don't keep me waiting. I gotta handle some business, but I'll text you later. Good night was all texted back.

I had no idea what the hell my dad wanted but this shit with Princeton was getting weirder by the day. Why the hell was this man meeting my father when I didn't even know shit about him my damn self? After putting my phone on the charger, I stripped out of my clothes and took a shower. Once I was done, I laid my clothes out for work then climbed into bed. I didn't even bother to put any clothes on. Before I knew it, I had drifted off to sleep.

Friday afternoon
Princeton

"I don't like the fact that you going over to meet her pops without me. You don't know that nigga," Perry bitched as we lifted weights at the gym.

"Bro, you know I'm not worried about that old nigga. If he comes at me wrong, I'll blow that nigga's head clear off his shoulders, so don't worry about me. You know I don't go anywhere without my heat. Besides, you know Tye and Bo gonna follow me to the house, so stop tripping." Perry just nodded in agreement but didn't say shit else.

Ty and Bo were my bodyguards and have been ever since I took my father's spot. They always had eyes on me. Perry had his own set of guards because the two of us weren't always together. After we left the gym, Perry and I decided to go to Wild Wings to grab some wings and fries. My cell rang and when I looked at the caller ID, it was some broad Lakeisha that I fucked around with when I needed to get my dick wet. Lakeisha was bad as shit but it was just sex for me. She had some good pussy but her ass was a hot girl and what I would call community pussy but I didn't care I always strapped up. Lakeisha didn't think I knew that she was out there but she had no idea how much I knew about her. All I'm going to say is she will never meet my mother. Hell, she not even worthy enough to be in the same state as my momma.

"Hey Lakiesha, wassup?"

"Hey, daddy. What you doing? You got time to break me off with that good dick?" she cooed into the phone getting straight to the point.

"Right now, I'm having lunch with my bro, but I should be free in about an hour, but I won't have a lot of time so as soon as we get in the door, just take your clothes off so I can hit you with this dick and send you on your way. Meet me at the spot in an hour," I told her before disconnecting the call. I didn't even give her a chance to respond. These bitches knew what it was for me.

"Nigga, we both about to be up in some pussy cause Shayla ass just asked for some dick. I ain't gonna lie; I can do without the pussy. I just want to fuck her mouth because her head game is A1. But I know she gonna want to fuck," Perry blurted. I just laughed at the nigga.

After we finished eating, we both went our separate ways. Twenty minutes later, I pulled up to my spot in Camden and Lakiesha was already there. This was the only spot any of the hoes I fucked with knew about because they would never step foot where I actually lay my head at.

"Damn daddy. You looking good in those baller shorts," she flirted.

"I'll look even better once I'm naked," I shot back. As soon as we walked in the door, Lakiesha dropped to her knees and blessed me with some fire head. I laid my head back against the wall and closed my eyes as I bit down on my bottom lip. Her warm, wet mouth felt so a good wrapped around my dick. She was sucking slow then fast. Lakiesha took her tongue and licked the head of my dick slowly then sped up. "Fuck girl! Suck that just like that," I groaned while gripping a handful of her hair.

I opened my eyes when Lakeshia removed her lips from my dick. She grabbed my hand and led me to the couch and pushed me down. I reached under the couch pillow and grabbed a rubber and put it on while she stripped out of her clothes. Once the condom was on, Lakiesha eased down onto my dick nice and slow. I lifted her up by her waist and shoved my dick into her.

"Oh shit, daddy," she moaned. Lakiesha matched me stroke for stroke.

"Cum on this dick," I demanded. I sucked her left breast in my mouth and flicked my tongue on her nipple causing her to cry out in ecstasy.

"Shit daddy, I'm about to cum," she moaned in my ear. Lakiesha was riding my dick like she was trying to make a baby until I felt her juices running down my manhood.

"Shit girl, I'm about to cum," I grunted as I let my load off in the condom. Lakiesha didn't get up right away; she just laid her head on my shoulder for a few seconds. I wiped the sweat off my forehead before lifting her body from mine.

"Damn, that shit was good, daddy." Lakeisha never called me by my name; she always called me daddy from the first day I hit it until now. Sometimes, I wondered if she actually knew my name, not that I really cared. I watched Lakiesha as she got dressed and I couldn't deny that she was a beauty. She was light-skinned with long red hair. She was a bit on the small side but she had a nice booty. As soon as Lakiesha left, I hopped in the shower and got dressed. It was almost time to see what in the hell did Goddess pops wanted to meet me for.

Friday evening

I shot Goddess a text letting her know that I was on my way. She wanted to drive herself but I wasn't having it. When I pulled to her house, she came out looking as beautiful as ever. I got out and opened the door for her. All I could do was shake my head because she was indeed a Goddess. The ride to her pops house was rather quiet and I was cool with that. I was going to break her out of all that.

Her pops lived in Mt Laurel and when I pulled up to his house, I knew he had some type of money because the outside alone was nice as hell. I got out of the car and walked around to let Goddess out. When we walked up, she punched in some code before the front door opened.

As soon as we got in the house, I couldn't lie and say that I wasn't impressed and was pretty eager to meet the man that owned this house. Some lady with an apron came out to greet us.

"Good evening Goddess and Mr. Princeton Hughes," the lady greeted me calling me by my first and last name. I needed to know how the fuck she knew my full name; I had never even told Goddess what my name was. She was wearing the same look of confusion that I was.

"Good evening, Ms. Sasha," Goddess replied back.

"Good evening," I spoke as she walked us toward the back of the house. As we walked through the house, I was really admiring the cream, gold, and white décor this man had going on. I thought my house was nice but my shit wouldn't be able to touch this on any level. We finally stopped once we reached the terrace where I assumed we would be having dinner at since there was a table full of food of all kinds of shit. It looked like he was about to feed a family of thirty people yet I only saw three plate settings.

"Good evening, Mr. Hughes. I'm Rashaad Jenkins, Goddess's father. It's a pleasure to meet the man that took a bullet for my baby girl," he spoke, looking me dead in the eyes with a firm handshake. I could tell right away that he was a real one. I had a feeling we were a lot alike and this would only go one of two ways. We were either gonna hit it off or hate one another. There was no in-between with men like him and me.

"It's a pleasure to meet you as well, Mr. Jenkins and for what it's worth, I'll take a million more bullets for your daughter," I told him holding the same type of energy that he held. Rashaad just looked at me for a few before speaking.

"I'm glad to hear that but let's eat and we can talk over dinner. I think it's time for the three of us to get acquainted," he stated. "Princess, what's wrong with you? It's not like you to be this quiet," Rashaad turned to Goddess and asked.

"I'm just trying to process what the hell is going on right now. All of this just feels a little weird, that's all," she answered sweetly.

"Baby girl, you already know your daddy more than any other person would ever know me so you're good, just relax and be yourself." Goddess just smiled before taking a seat across from me. Her pops blessed the food and we dug in. I was fucking that food up; his cook was the bomb.

"Dad, this food is really good tonight, especially these ribs. Are you enjoying the food?" Goddess turned to me and asked.

"Yeah, this food is everything. Your cook is the bomb," I told Rashaad.

"That's why she's been working for me for ten years. Now, let me get to the point to why I called y'all here. I know that my daughter is really into you although she knows nothing about you. The reason I know is that I raised her myself without the help of her mother. And the fact that she let you eat her pussy in a bathroom while her boyfriend was in the other room says a lot," he said, shocking the shit out of me that he even knew that. I spit my damn drink; that's how caught off guard I was.

"There's only two type of women that would do some shit like that, a hoe or a woman who has a strong connection that she can't shake. And I know she isn't a hoe so it has to be the second one," Rashaad stated confidently. "Because I know I didn't raise no hoes."

"Dad!" she yelped and I thought it was the cutest thing the way she said his name.

"Goddess, don't act new; you know I don't hold my tongue and I ain't gonna start tonight. But I'm going to say this: I know that you're gonna give him a shot but before you do, I think there are some things that you need to know and I'm gonna let him tell you," her pops stated and I had no idea what the fuck he was talking about. Goddess looked at me with a confused expression and I'm sure I was wearing the same one while looking at her pops.

"With all due respect, Mr. Jenkins, I don't know what you are referring to," I spoke up.

"Tell my daughter what you do for a living?"

"I'm a kingpin and a ruthless killer when I'm fucked with or fucked over. That's what I do," I spoke proudly about my job like that shit was legal. I looked at Goddess and I could tell that she was shocked to hear me say that but it was the truth. She looked a little hurt by my confession.

"You're a drug dealer? But you were at business dinner," Goddess quizzed with confusion laced in her voice.

"First and foremost, I'm not a drug dealer, I'm the kingpin. I supply the drug dealers. And yes, I was at a business meeting and I supply damn near everyone that was in attendance." Her mouth dropped open so wide that I could see the back of her throat.

"Wow, I can't believe this shit," Goddess mumbled. It was time for me to find out how this nigga knew so much of my business.

"So, Mr. Jenkins, how do you know so much of my business?" I asked.

"I'm glad that you asked. After doing my research after the shooting, I found out your last name and did a little more digging and realized that you were the son of non-other than Curtis Hughes. One of the biggest kingpins there was. Your daddy and I go way back. He was the only nigga in the business that I fucked with. You probably don't remember me but I remember you and your little brother Perry and your mother. Your daddy was the reason I'm where I'm at today. He used to call me Street Legend. Your pops took me under his wings when I first got in the game. I respected your father very much and was fucked up when he got murked."

I stood there speechless and immediately remembered hearing that name in my house. "Wait, you're THE Rashaad Jenkins?" I inquired.

"The one and only," he replied proudly.

"This is a small world. Who would've have thought that my future father-in-law was a good friend of my father's?" I threw out. Goddess's pops just snickered but didn't say anything.

"There is no way I would ever date you knowing what I know now. I work at a school. What the hell do I look like dating a street nigga?" she blurted. I just sighed and rubbed my hands down my face.

"Daddy, you could have told me what he did for a living with just the two of us," she stated.

"Yeah, I could've but I wanted to look him in his face and be in his presence to see what type of man he was. I can't lie, I'm impressed. He's a real man regardless of his profession. I can't knock him for doing the same shit that took care of my children. I know that in the event you decided to be with him, he'll protect you at all cost and provide. So, he's okay with me. I have no reason to believe that he would kill anything that comes up against you, myself included, and that's the type of man that I trust with my daughters."

"This is too much. I'm ready to go," Goddess blurted.

"Goddess, wait," I called after her but she never looked back.

"Let her go, she needs some time to herself. She'll be okay. Besides, I wanna wrap with you alone," her pops told me.

"Wassup?" I asked and no sooner than the words left my lips, that nigga's fist connected with my jaw. I was shocked as shit, but I punched that nigga back and we went a couple of rounds in a full fight before he finally stopped throwing blows. I couldn't lie, that old nigga had hands; my jaw was killing me.

"Yo', why the fuck did you hit me?" I yelled.

"I needed to make sure you could fight with your hands in case you have to protect my daughter and can't get to your gun. My princess can't date no pussy nigga. But I'm glad to see that you can fight. You can go now, I'm about to get up in some pussy," Rashaad said with a wide smile. This was some interesting, crazy shit but for some odd reason, I liked how her father rolled.

"That shit wasn't necessary, she already said she wasn't fucking with me like that," I blurted.

"Remember this son, anything worth having is worth fighting for and my daughter is without a doubt worth having." I just nodded then got the hell out of there.

CHAPTER 4

Rashaad

I had just landed in Atlanta about an hour ago. It was time to do a pop-up visit at one of my clubs. It's been a little over four months since I came to see what was going on myself. When I walked in my club, my fine ass bartender was bent over putting away some liquor. Shantae was fine as shit with some good pussy. She and I fucked around every time I came to Atlanta. It was something about her that I really liked but we just kept our relationship basic. I came to town and we hooked up, but once I left, she was out of sight, out of mind. Shantae and I have been fucking around for about three years now.

"Let me find out that ass getting bigger," I stated. Shantae got up with her hands on her hips about to rip me a new one until she saw who I was.

"Oh my God, Rashaad! It's so good to see you," she said, hugging me tightly. The smell of her perfume was breathtaking and I didn't want to let her go. I placed a kiss on her neck and palmed her ass with my hands. Shantae was about 5'5 and with a nice little body. She was brown-skinned with a cute face and she wore her hair cut short for as long as I could remember but it fit her face nicely.

"You know it's always a pleasure to see you, Shantae. You're looking good as usual," I told her while twirling her around.

"Well, thank you, sir. I don't have to tell you that you're looking pretty dapper yourself," she replied. "So, what brings you here tonight?"

"I'm just coming to make sure shit is running correctly and of course, you know I want to chill with you while I'm here."

"Oh, is that right? Well, we can do that. As far as business go, I'm not going to hold you. It's been kinda slow in here for the last few weeks. We still making money but not as much as we normally bring in. I just think that Kenny's ass is starting to slip but you didn't hear that from me," Shantae stated.

"You know I'll never repeat what you say to me, but I need to take care of some business. I'll be back tonight. But let's keep the fact that I'm in town our little secret for now," I told her.

"Okay, no problem. I'll see your sexy ass later," she flirted.

Once I left the club, I headed back to my hotel room. No matter how hard I tried I couldn't get Shantae off my mind, which was weird. I poured myself a drink and lit a cigar as I stood on the balcony taking in the view. It was Friday evening and the sun was starting to set. I called my man Money up and told him to come chill with me at the club tonight. After deciding on what to wear, I hopped in the shower to wash my day off. I grabbed my lotion and lotioned my body before putting on my boxers. I decided to wear a grey blazer with a white t-shirt, black jeans, and a pair of grey-and-white Jordans. After throwing on my jewelry and my oil that had me smelling godly, I was ready to go.

Knock knock!!

When I got to the door, it was the girls. They wanted to tag along and I thought it would be fun to have my daughters and niece come to one of my clubs.

"Hey daddy," Goddess spoke cheerfully as usual.

"Hey, Princesses," I greeted the three of them placing kisses on all three of their cheeks.

"Damn, uncle Shad, you threw that shit on tonight. Let me find out you tryna catch something tonight," my niece Latrice stated. I took in the girls looks for the first time in a long time and both of my daughters looked so much like their mother. Andrea was a beauty; she was high yellow with long, jet-black hair down to the middle of her back. She was every man's dream girl but she was also available for the highest bidder. I wasn't quite sure when she got like that but it is what is. I just couldn't believe how she really up and left her kids and never came back. Sometimes I wondered if she was even alive. Because that just wasn't like her. Although it was short-lived and probably don't seem like it now but Andrea loved those girls to death.

"Dad, you good? You done zoned out on us," Journey asked.

"My bad, but yeah, I'm good. Honestly, I was just taking in y'all beauty and it made me think about y'all mom. Y'all ready to roll?"

"We sure are because I'm ready to party," Goddess blurted.

"Y'all better not get too drunk if y'all planning to drive because I already have plans tonight. So I suggest you catch an Uber or something."

When I pulled up to the club, it was packed outside just the way that I liked it. That means I was making money. The girls and I walked in the club through the back entrance. I put them in VIP and told them to have fun. I went in my office and checked some emails and looked at some paperwork. It was clear to me that somebody was dipping in something they had no business dipping into which meant I was gonna have to fuck somebody up tonight because I didn't play around about my money or my daughters. I figured I'll handle that shit tomorrow when I called a meeting. I walked out the office and just observed what was going on. As I stood, the MC made an announcement.

"We have a mother fucking celebrity in the building! My nigga Tip, better known as TI, is here chilling in the building tonight." Screams from the crowd was crazy. I just smiled to myself and made way over to the girls that seemed to be enjoying themselves before I went to sit at the bar and rap with Shantae.

"Hey beautiful," I said when she came to take my drink order.

"Hello handsome. You're looking mighty good. Will you be having your usual?" I just nodded with a smile. I wasn't sure if I was tripping or not but something felt a little different than the other times when I hook up with her.

"I can't wait to get you alone tonight. I want you to spend the night with me then let me take you out to breakfast," I stated catching her off guard. Hell, I caught myself off guard. Besides some flirting and our little flings, Shantae never spent the night with me and I damn sure ain't never taken her out to eat. I was tripping or lonely one. After about two drinks, I made my way to the front of the club and made my way to the stage.

"Oh shit, we got none other than the owner of this bitch in the house! Everybody, make some noise for the owner of this club, my man, Rashaad!" I walked up on the stage like the king I was and the ladies started going crazy. I was eating that shit up.

"Give my ass something to dance to," I yelled, feeling myself. Once the beat dropped, I did an old school two-step to get the crowd hype. "All jokes aside, anybody that knows me, know I like to have fun. But I just wanted to bless y'all with my presence and thank each and every one of you for coming out to Lucky Charms. I hope y'all having fun but don't forget to pay the lovely bartender over there a visit because she makes the best damn drinks in Atlanta!" I yelled to the crowd.

Goddess

I had to admit that my dad's club here in Atlanta was popping. Then, TI came and blessed us with his presence really causing the crowd to go wild. My sister, cousin and I were fucking the club up. That was the one thing the three of us could do was dance. I definitely was gonna need an Uber because I was feeling it. I was up dancing when I thought my eyes were playing tricks on me. I looked up and Princeton and a few other guys were in the VIP booth across from us. I think my heart stopped then started up again. I couldn't lie, that man was as fine as they come. He looked at me but never once did he acknowledge me and for some strange reason, that put me in my feelings. I guess I couldn't blame him. I haven't seen or heard from him since the night we were at my dad's house. I ignored all of his calls and told the front desk to tell him I wasn't in the office when he came by. I guess he got tired of chasing me so he stopped.

"I can't believe that Princeton is here and looked me right in my face and didn't even speak," I blurted talking to Journey and Latrice.

"Don't look right now, but right over there." They both looked and Latrice looked as if she was amazed.

"Damn bitch, that's Princeton? Please tell me why the fuck you not dating him again? And why are you so mad about him not speaking? Aren't you the one that pushed him away?" she stated. Her words cut me deep and I didn't know why because it was the truth. I didn't want him. At least that's what I had convinced myself into believing. I just rolled my eyes at her because I didn't feel like talking about him right now.

As hard as I tried not to look over at his booth, I just couldn't help it, but I wished I had never looked. There was a chick sitting on Princeton's lap and he had his hand wrapped around her waist. She leaned over and whispered in his ear and the way he was smiling infuriated me. I wasn't sure if it was the liquor or my true feelings that were coming to surface, but I was really in my bag and I was ready to show my ass even if I ended up looking stupid.

"I'm going over there," I told them as I headed towards his booth.

"Goddess, I don't think that's a good idea," Journey warned but against my better judgment, I went anyway. I walked over to Princeton's booth and we locked eyes but yet, he still wouldn't acknowledge me.

"So, you're just gonna act like you don't see me standing here, Princeton?" I yelled.

Everyone that was in the booth got quiet and turned their attention to me. Princeton stared at me for a few seconds then shook his head.

"I don't know who you are, but I need to speak to him in private," I slurred, talking to the girl that was sitting on his lap. Princeton laughed which caused everyone else to laugh. I was getting irritated by the second.

"So, you gone really sit here and disrespect me, Princeton?" I asked getting a little emotional. I was fucking tripping and I knew it but I just didn't know how to stop. At this point, Journey and Latrice was standing beside me trying to pull my hand to make me leave.

"Come on, Goddess. Let's go. Apparently he don't want to talk to you, so don't force him. You making a scene and you better than this," Journey argued.

"Yeah, listen to your girl," Princeton replied.

"You know what? You're right, let's go. Fuck you, Princeton and that hoe you're showing off for." Princeton looked at me angrily and damn near pushed the girl that was sitting on his lap to the floor.

"Fuck me, Goddess? You mad that I stopped chasing your fucking snooty ass after trying to make you my fucking woman for damn near two months and you played me the fuck out no matter what I did? Now you want to come ruin my night because you see some chick on my lap?" he yelled. "Then you have the nerve to be drunk and shit embarrassing yourself and me. You got some fucking nerve. I haven't seen or heard from your ass in three months and suddenly you feel like you entitled to pull this shit! I really think you should go, Goddess!" he yelled. As angry as he was and no matter how loud he was shouting, I could tell that Princeton still wanted me. I guess the liquor made me face my truth because as hurt as my feelings were, not to mention, I was embarrassed, I realized at that moment I was just as into him as he was into me and I was about to let it be known.

"Princeton, I'm sorry for coming at you like that but seeing you with that girl had me feeling some type of way. I thought about you every day and was just too stubborn to give in. But I don't care anymore. I want to give us a shot. The thought of what could be is killing me, but I understand if you're not into me anymore I had to speak my truth. I would like to get to know you," I stated, feeling my emotions take over and I felt a single tear fall from my eyes. The room was silent as I heard the girl that was on his lap suck her teeth and I wanted to punch her in her face.

Princeton's face softened a little bit; he shook his head before walking towards me. I didn't know what he was about to say or do so the nerves in my stomach were doing backflips.

"It's about fucking time you came to your senses. Now, let me get you outta here so you can lay down. You drunk as fuck, ma. I'm taking her with me," he told Journey.

"Goddess, are you sure you want to go with him?" Journey asked. I just nodded my head and walked off with Princeton. The ride to his hotel seemed long as hell, but it was silent and felt like everything was spinning. When we got to his room, I barely made it in the door before I was throwing up everywhere.

"Fuck Goddess," Princeton said before helping me to a trash can. I felt like shit. I was dizzy and my head was pounding. This was a mess, I was a mess.

The next morning

When I woke up, I panicked. I was in a t-shirt in an unfamiliar room. I looked around and realized that I was by myself and wondered how the hell did I get here and where were my clothes I got up to use the bathroom and as I was walking out, I heard the door open. When I looked up it was Princeton. I thought I was tripping but then I did remember running into him at the club.

"Princeton, what am I doing here? Oh my God! Did we sleep together?" I blurted.

"Good morning to you, too, Goddess. So, you don't remember how you got here and if we had sex?" he quizzed, giving me the side-eye. I put my head down shamefully before answering.

"Honestly, I don't," I told him.

"Well, to answer your first question, I brought you here because you were drunk, jealous, and started showing your ass. So after you confessed your feelings for me, we came back here and I fucked the shit out of you until you fell asleep," Princeton blurted causing my mouth to drop open. I felt so stupid how I could I allow that to happen.

"I can't believe that I did that," I told him shaking my head.

"That's why you shouldn't be drinking like that. If you can't handle your liquor then don't drink. But all jokes aside, everything I said to you was true except us fucking. We didn't fuck. Your clothes were missing because you threw up everywhere. But understand this, when I put this pipe in you, you'll remember. I wouldn't give a damn if you were in a coma," he boasted.

"Oh my God, you play too damn much," I told Princeton I couldn't help but to laugh because he had got me good.

"Here, take these clothes and go shower and get dressed. I'm about to take you to breakfast but make sure you text your fam and let the know you're good."

CHAPTER 5

Princeton

erry and I decided to go to Atlanta to visit my mother for about a week. I missed my mother dearly and couldn't wait to spend time with her. That Friday night, we decided to hit up some club called Lucky Charms. We heard from our cousins that was the turn-up spot in the big A so that's where I wanted to be. When we got to the club, that shit was popping with a big ass crowd. We headed up to VIP and immediately started popping bottles. I was feeling nice and chilling with some chick that I had met when I walked in. She was a cutie with a nice little body so I figured I'll chill with her for a bit and get my dick wet at the end of the night. I thought I was tripping when the DJ announced that the owner of the club was in the building and called up Goddess' father to the stage. I liked Rashaad he was a cool dude and I could see why my father fucked with him. I had planned to make my way to see him before leaving but thanks to his daughter that didn't happen. My eyes damn near popped out of my head when I saw Goddess over in the VIP across from us. We locked eyes and I just put my head down because I wasn't fucking with her. I had chased her ass hard since the day we left her pops house and she made it clear she didn't want me. I was surprised at myself that I was dick riding a chick because I had never put that much effort into a woman before. I could have any woman I wanted and I meant that literally. Baby girl from the club was sitting on my lap chilling and making plans for the night when I looked up and saw that Goddess was making her way over.

I couldn't believe how she was acting in this club then I quickly realized that she had to be drinking because she had some damn nerve interrupting me because she was in her feelings. When she first came over, I didn't pay her ass any mind and that's when she got in her feelings and embarrassed the both of us. I wasn't really the type guy to disrespect a woman, but I was ready to curse her ass out. I would be lying if I said when she told baby to excuse herself didn't turn me on, but I was still pissed, nevertheless. Once Goddess started talking, I softened up and took my ass back to my room. Just because I was pissed at her didn't mean I wasn't still feeling her. When we got to the room, her drunk ass threw up every damn where leaving me to clean it up. After getting her together, I put Goddess in one of my shirts then we both took our asses to sleep. The next morning, I ran out to go get her something to put on and when I got back to the room, she was coming from the bathroom. Goddess looked so beautiful even with her disheveled hair. When she asked if we had sex, I had to fuck with her and tell her yeah. She damned near died.

I waited for her to get dressed so I could take her to breakfast so we could talk. I needed to see where her head was at now that she was sober. When we got to the Waffle House, we looked over the menu then ordered. I wasn't about to play around with her so I got straight to the point.

"So, Goddess, wassup? You ready to be my woman or what?" I blurted catching her off guard. She was quiet for a brief moment before answering my question.

"I mean, I'm ready to date you and get to know you. I want to take things one day at a time," Goddess stated.

"You sure that's all you want to be? Because last night you bossed up on a nigga and was making demands like you were my wife and shit. But listen, I don't ever want to see you out drunk like that. It's nothing cute or attractive about a drunken woman. I don't care how beautiful she is," I told her honestly. "I'm not trying to be mean or nothing, but I'm not into drunken women. I like you a lot Goddess and I can't wait to spend time and get to know you. But before we start, I need to tell you a few things about me outside of what you already know so you'll know what you're getting into with me. For starters, I'm a very jealous man. What's mine is mine and that's that. Secondly, I don't deal with disrespect of no kind from anyone of any sorts. Thirdly, my family and money are everything to me and I'll kill anyone or thing that fucks with either one.

I can be a piece of work, Goddess and I live a dangerous lifestyle, but I will always do my best to protect you at all cost. No one really fucks with me because they know how the Hughes' get down. There is always someone willing to try you, mostly out of jealousy. I want to keep you in the light yet in the dark at the same time about my lifestyle if that makes sense. I don't ever want you caught up in my shit, but I do want you to know how I get down. And as long as you're cool with what I said, I think we'll be great. That was just a few things but there's so much more to me but you'll have to find out those things along the way. Is there any key things I need to know about you?" I quizzed. I was the type of guy that got straight to the point and didn't sugar coat a damn thing. I was as real as they come.

"I can be a little mouthy at times, I don't have no filter, and although I'm not into anything illegal, I know a lot about it. My father always kept it real with us and taught my sister and I everything there was to know about the game. I know how to protect myself and I too don't play around when it comes to my family. My dad and sister mean everything to me," she answered, taking a sip of her orange juice.

"Well, that's good to know, but I can handle that. So, after knowing those key things about me, you still fucking with a nigga or what?" I asked getting straight to the point. She just simply nodded her head yes. That was cool with me. I was trying to keep cool and act like this shit wasn't a big deal but deep down, I wanted to do a few backflips right there in the Waffle House.

"Let's get out of here. I need to meet up with my brother and cousins in a few. I came up to visit my mom. I've been here for about a week, but I'm leaving tomorrow. Your dad's club was the talk of Atlanta but I had no clue your pops owned it until he got called to the stage. To say I was surprised to see him let alone you, would be an understatement."

"Yeah, I was definitely shocked to see you. This is the second time I went out of town and ran into you. What are the odds? Was starting to think you had a tracker on me," Goddess said with a giggle.

"You funny as hell. I like a woman with a sense of humor," I told her. She just smiled and that was the first time I had completely taken in her beauty. Goddess was like a bronze complexion with deep dimples and a beautiful smile. After talking for a little while longer, I dropped her off at her hotel which was up from where I was staying.

"If you came to visit your mom, why didn't you stay with her?" she asked out of the blue.

"Because I planned to get some ass, while I was here and would never bring any of those skanks to my momma's house not that she would allow it anyway," I answered honestly. Goddess facial expression let me know that she didn't like my answer.

"So, you've had sex since you've been here?" she quizzed.

"Not that I owe you an explanation being as though I'm a single man that weren't even talking to you at the time but if you must know, yes, I've had some pussy since I've been here. I'm a man with needs and no woman so what did expect to happen? Look, don't start tripping on me, Goddess. It's not that deep," I told her.

"You're right and I'm good. Enjoy the rest of your visit with your mom and I'll talk to you later," she replied before exiting the car. I knew she wasn't good but I wasn't about to baby her over something I did before I even started talking to her ass.

When I walked in my mom's crib, she was sitting in the living room watching the news.

"Hey momma, wassup? What you trying to do today? You know we have an early flight so I wanna spend as much time with you today as possible," I told her.

"Princeton, I told you and your brother that we didn't have to go anywhere and we could just chill here but leave it to my damn boys to be hardheaded," she fussed.

"Mom, why you always fussing about shit we wanna do for you and where the hell is your son?" I quizzed, realizing that Perry wasn't here yet.

"Hell if I know. He texted me about a half-hour ago and said he was on his way, so how you beat him here beats me and ain't no damn body fussing." A few minutes later, Perry's ass walked in smiling and shit.

"Nigga, where the hell was you at?" I quizzed.

"I was chilling, where the hell was you at since you want to be all up in my business."

"I was chilling that's what I was doing," I shot back.

For the rest of the day, we sat and chilled with my mom. That night, my aunt and a few of my cousins came through. My mom cooked for us while we had a few drinks and played spades. I missed my mom like crazy and was thinking about asking her to move back home. I even thought about moving here with her. We chilled and played cards into the wee hours of the night until we got tired. My mom turned in about an hour before we did. We didn't even bother to go back to the hotel, we just crashed at my mom's crib. The next morning when I woke up, I smelled food and made my way to the kitchen. Perry's greedy ass was already at the damn table.

"Good morning mom," I greeted, placing a kiss on her cheek.

"Good morning, baby." After we ate, we stayed for about another hour before heading back to the hotel to get our belongings. I realized that I hadn't talked to Goddess since I dropped her off. I made a mental note to hit her up once I got back to Jersey.

****

We didn't even have time to take our shit home because we had a meeting as soon as we got back. When I walked into the warehouse where we sometimes hold our meetings at, a few of my buyers looked uneasy and I wasn't beat to deal with no bullshit right now but it was gonna be what it was gonna be.

"Wassup, y'all? Why y'all looking crazy and shit?" I asked getting straight to the point.

"I don't know what the fuck is going on but someone hit two of our trap houses in the same week, both a day after shipment. The crazy thing is they only took the weight and no money. We didn't want to bother y'all while y' all was on vacation," this little nigga Ricky answered. I rubbed my hands down my face and took a deep breath before responding. I knew if I didn't think first, I would need a clean-up crew cause I would start laying niggas down without a second thought.

"I don't know what the fuck,y'all saying but all I know is y'all have three days to find out who took my shit and once you find out, bring them to me personally. If I don't have my shit back or my money, I'm gonna start dropping bodies. I know ain't nobody crazy enough to come for us. But I'm tired and need a nap. So, meeting dismissed unless you have something to say, Perry?"

Nah, I'm straight. Let's be out," he said before we headed out the door. When we got outside, something seemed a little off and I didn't feel right.

Pow, pow, pow!!

Bullets rang out. I reached for my gun and started bussing off. Something was off with this entire situation. *"Who the hell knew we were gonna be here today?"* I thought as I popped a nigga in his skull. I couldn't believe we were in a fucking shootout in the middle of the day. Eventually, the shooting came to an end as the bodies were laid out. I don't know who the fuck sent these amateurs but they forgot to tell them who the fuck they were dealing with. I caught a glimpse of one of the other shooters still breathing so I walked over to him and aimed my gun at his head.

"Who the fuck sent you?" I yelled.

"Tommy," he answered just before he took his last breath. All though I knew he was dead already, anger took over my body and I shot his ass in the head anyway. I didn't know who the hell Tommy was, but I needed to find out and fast. When I looked up, the cleanup crew was there. I didn't even bother to go home because I needed to have another brief meeting. Once the meeting was over, I pulled Perry to the side so we could talk right quick.

"Yo', that nigga that I shot in the head told me somebody named Tommy sent them just before he took his last breath. Who the fuck is Tommy? I didn't mention that shit in the meeting because whomever he is has inside help and I don't want them to know that we're on to their asses. So, I'm gonna keep the team out the loop until we connect the dots then lullaby their asses."

"Yeah cause this shit is crazy as hell but they fucking with the wrong ones," Perry responded.

"Look, I'm out and I'm going to my main crib tonight." I needed to clear my head.

"Aight cool. I'ma head home, too. This shit got a nigga head fucked up. I need a blunt," he said.

I had already texted my security coverage. I told him he could have the day off since it was Sunday and we were just getting back but little did I know this shit was gonna happened. It looks like I'm gonna have to have a security detail at all times.

When I got in the house, I stripped out of my clothes and hit the shower. I let the hot water cascade down my body as my mind wandered off to another place. I had so much shit on my mind at once. I had just the right thing to help ease it for the time being. As soon as I got out the shower, I lit a blunt. I didn't even bother to put clothes on. When I finished smoking, I decided to call Goddess and see what she was up to. She answered the phone on the first ring sounding sexy as shit.

"Hello," she answered.

"Hey wassup, baby. How are you feeling?" I asked.

"I'm good, just a little tired. I decided to take a day off from work to just chill. How about you, what are you up to?

"Not much. Just got out the shower about to take a nap then get up and find something to eat. I just wanted to hear your voice before I went to sleep, but I'll hit you up when I wake up."

"Aww, aren't' you sweet? Well, get some rest. I might take a nap myself," Goddess replied.

For the next hour, I tossed and turned thinking about the shit that took place earlier. Why did I always have to kill a nigga? I just wanted to get money and live. Killing wasn't something I enjoyed doing but it was damn sure something I would do without thinking twice. My thoughts weren't getting me anywhere at the moment and I really needed some sleep. I finally felt my body drifting off into a deep sleep.

Journey

"Hey baby, you're looking good in that dress," my baby said placing a kiss on my neck.

"You looking good yourself," I told him.

It's been two months since I met my new love back in Atlanta. I haven't told anyone about him yet and I wasn't sure why. I feel kinda bad for keeping this secret from my sister and my dad but mainly my sister. I wasn't sure how she would feel when I told her or if she would even care for that manner. On our way to dinner, I noticed his driver kept looking around watching his surroundings. It made me kinda paranoid but I tried to stay calm but my instincts told me that something wasn't right.

"Boss, I think we have trouble," his driver Rob stated.

"Baby, I need you to do exactly as I say. I need you to get all the way down on the floor and stay there until further instruction," my love stated. I did as I was told and got all the way down. No sooner as I hit the floor, shots rang out. The car was swerving all over the road like some shit you see on TV. Although I was scared as shit, I was also turned on watching my boo in action. The shooting finally came to an end. When I didn't hear anything, I hoped like hell neither of them were hit or dead.

"Rob, you good?" he asked but there was no response. My heart was pounding faster than it already was.

"I need to get to the spot. I was hit," Rob finally said. I heard my boo make a call. He was talking in code, but I could pretty much understand what he was saying.

"Baby, are you good?" he finally asked me.

"Yes, I'm good. Are you?"

"Yeah, I'm good, baby. I have to drop you off but I'll pick you up later if you sill fucking with a nigga."

"Why wouldn't I be? Just be careful," I told him. Once I got in the house, I decided to call my sister. I think it was time that we talked.

"Hey Journey. I was just thinking about you," she sang into the phone.

"Are you busy because I really need to talk to you?"

"I'll be right over. Are you good?" Goddess quizzed.

"Yes, I'm fine."

"Aight, I'm on my way." A few minutes later, my sister was standing in my living room.

"What's up, sis?"

"Listen, I don't know why I haven't said anything until now, but I've been kicking it with Perry for the last two month: Since the night at the club in Atlanta," I told her. Goddess stared at me for a few before laughing. I didn't see shit funny so I was looking at her like she was crazy.

"What the hell is so funny, Goddess?"

"Bitch, I been knew that. I was just waiting for you to tell me. At first, I was upset because I wanted to know why the hell did you see the need to keep some shit like that a secret and from me of all people. But that's your business. I'm happy for you."

"How the hell did you know?" I quizzed.

"Girl, you started acting all weird and sneakily. Smiling when you texted then you started being missing in action at the same time he was missing. Besides, nothing gets pass Princeton. By the way, your daddy knows, too," she stated and my mouth dropped open.

"Oh my God," I said while laughing. "But look, something happened today that kinda scared me," I told her changing the subject.

"What's wrong?"

"Today we were in a shootout and his driver was hit in the shoulder. I was scared and turned on at the same time. The crazy thing was, I could feel that something was about to happen, but I tried to ignore it."

"Damn, that's crazy as hell. Are you okay?" Goddess asked.

"I know right and yes, I'm good. I was just a little shaken up."

"Look, I know you don't want to but we need to tell daddy. You know he'll tell us how to handle ourselves in those types of situations. I know we know how to defend ourselves but we never really had to," she stated making a good point.

"Maybe you're right but you know he probably about to blow a head gasket when he hears about the shootout. Well, let's go get this over with," I mumbled.

When we got to my dad's house, he was just pulling up in his driveway so we pulled up right behind him.

"Hey, girls. What brings y'all pass my house? Are y'all good?"

"Hey dad. Yeah, we good but we do want to talk to you," I told him. my dad didn't say anything; he just opened the door and walked in the house. When we got in, he poured himself a drink and sat down.

"Aight, what's going on?" I swallowed the lump that was in my throat before speaking, but I guess I was still taking too long because Goddess blurted out what I was trying to say before I could.

"First, she finally told me that she was dealing with Perry and secondly, she was with him today and a car started shooting at them and his driver was hit." My dad still didn't say anything; he just pulled on his beard hair.

"What happened to my little girls? Y'all both fucking with street niggas when y'all could have easily landed yourselves doctors, lawyers, or any other respectable profession but nope, y'all didn't want that. I try to mind my business when it comes to your love life. Don't get me wrong, I like Princeton and Perry but their lifestyle is dangerous and as long as y'all are dating them, y'all lives will be in danger. I can't knock their hustle because I used to be a street nigga. Now I'm legit but I still have a street mentality so I'll still shoot first and ask questions later especially when it comes to the two of you. That includes y'all men. I will kill them without thinking twice if something happens to my girls behind their shit. Now I have to involve myself. I need to speak to them both ASAP like right now. Get y'all niggas on the phone and tell them to get their asses here," he demanded. He was kinda scaring me. I let Goddess call Princeton to deliver the message. I didn't feel like it was a reason for both of us to call them.

"They'll be here in like a half-hour."

"Cool, I have some shit to handle in my office until they get here. After you buzz them in, let me know," my dad stated before going into his office. I had no idea what was about to happen, but I think shit was about to get real because the one thing I knew for certain was my dad didn't play when it came to me and my sister. Sometimes he seemed over the top but I would probably be the same way if I had kids. He always told us we wouldn't understand until we had our own.

Princeton

E ver since the night I ran into Goddess at the club we've been inseparable. She's been everything I thought she would be and more. Sometimes it felt like we've been together forever and it's only been two months. Believe it or not, we still haven't had sex yet and it was mainly on my part. But I knew once I put this pipe in Goddess, I was gonna get possessive and wouldn't let her go. This was the first time I ever did that shit so I knew she was special to a nigga. Usually, I'll fuck a chick before knowing her name and if the pussy was good and I planned to hit it again, then I would learn the basics about them and nothing more. But with Goddess, I wanted to know everything imaginable about her and some before sexing her. Perry and I had just left the warehouse after he told me about the shit that went down with him and Rob while Journey was with them. It was crazy how he thought he was keeping a secret bout him and my girl's sister. We put that shit together a while back. Shit was crazy and we were still getting hit with no idea who had it out for us or why but I was getting sick of the shit and ready for this to be over with. I felt my phone vibrating in my pocket and when I looked at the phone it was my baby Goddess

"Hey baby, wassup?" I answered.

"Um, nothing much," I could tell that she was lying and that she wanted something by the tone of her voice.

"Don't do that shit, Goddess. Wassup?"

"I'm over at my dad's house and he wants to see you and Perry ASAP," she said into the phone. I sighed heavily before responding.

"Aight yo'. I'll be there in about a half-hour or so," I said then hung up.

I wasn't trying to be rude with her or nothing but I wasn't in the mood for her to be pussyfooting about what she wanted and I damn sure wasn't beat for her dad's fuckery. I already had a long day.

"Wassup bro? You look a little pissed," Perry asked.

"I am pissed. Goddess dad wants to talk to both of us and I know he about to be on some bullshit."

"That nigga bet not come at me sideways or I'm gonna lay his ass out today, but let's go see what that nigga want," Perry barked.

When I pulled up near the house, I called Goddess so she could let me in the gate. After parking, we walked up to the door where Goddess was waiting. Even though she had me a little pissed on the phone, the minute my eyes landed on her sexy ass all that shit went out the window. I pulled her in for a hug and kissed her lips.

"Wassup fellas? Can I get you something to drink?" Rashaad asked.

"I'll take some Henny."

"I'll take the same," Perry replied as well. After he poured our liquor, we all sat down.

"So, I'm just gonna get to the point and Perry, I start with you first since you thought it was okay to fuck my daughter for two months without meeting me first. When a woman is special to you and you fucking with a street nigga's daughter, you have enough respect to come to him like a man before you dick her down," he barked. All I could do was shake my head because this nigga had no kind of chill or filter. I knew that Perry wasn't gonna like that shit though.

"Yo', with all due respect, I'm a grown-ass man and don't need your permission to stick my dick anywhere. How the hell was I supposed to know your daughter was gonna be special when she let me hit the first night?" he spat but I could tell that he instantly regretted it. The room fell silent and Journey got up off the couch. I could see the hurt in her eyes. My brother was definitely out of line with that shit. The next thing I knew, Journey smacked the shit out of Perry. "So, that's how you feel, Perry? Fuck you!" she yelled before storming off into another room. Goddess got up to follow her.

"If you ever speak of my daughter that way again, I'll blast your ass right where you stand and that's a promise."

"My bad. I didn't mean it like that I was outta line. I apologize, sir, but please, don't threaten me again; I don't take to kind to threats."

"Good but I can assure that wasn't a threat so do what you need to do. Girls, come back in here so I can get to the point so y'all can get this disrespectful nigga outta my house." When they walked back in Journey looked like she was crying. I was ready to go. All of this shit was getting on my fucking nerves, but I did what to hear what he had to say. Journey was giving Perry the death stare.

"Look, just by the events that just happened today, I can tell that either of you have ever been serious about a woman before and only used to watching your own backs. Well, now that y'all have women, you have to watch their backs, too. All day, every day. You know why? Because the enemy becomes infatuated with the ones you love the most. Who's ever out to get y'all will soon be out to get my girls. And if y'all can't protect them, then leave them. Because if I get that phone call that every parent dreads getting, I'm gonna have to bury you. I'm not saying this just to say it. This little incident today was no accident and they are gonna hit again and each time is gonna get harder until you kill the head nigga in charge."

Rashaad had my full attention because this was shit I never considered. Plus, he was an OG so he had to know what he was talking about and he was a good friend of my pops and he was full of wisdom. I never thought about making sure my girl had car detail for when she wasn't with me. I was starting to feel like less of a man that I hadn't about that. Then, Journey could have been killed today. Suddenly something clicked.

"Do you know of anyone by the name of Tommy?" I quizzed.

"I know a few, why do you ask?

"Because a couple of months ago some of my shit was stolen and then there was a shooting at my warehouse and just before I killed one of the guys, I asked who sent him and he said Tommy, but I don't know who the fuck that is," I stated.

"The only Tommy I know that might be salty enough to do some shit like that would be Tommy Wick. He used to be jealous over your dad's position and he wanted your momma," Rashaad stated. "But I haven't heard that name in years. Didn't think the nigga was still alive. Y'all don't have beef with no one else?" he quizzed.

"Not that we know of but it could be anybody in this game," Perry stated.

"Y'all just fucked my head up. Now I'm gonna have to do some digging. I'll have some info in a few days. Come back Wednesday around 6 pm so I can let y'all know what I found out and to finish this chat."

"Aight thanks, Mr. Shad."

"No thanks needed. Girls, stick around for a second. I need to talk to y'all alone. They'll be right out," he turned to me and said.

When Perry and I got outside, all I could think about was everything that Rashaad had said to us. He may not have had the greatest delivery but he meant well and I didn't blame him for going crazy over his girls. I had no idea what it was like to have a kid of my own, but I'll be just as crazy over mine if not more. I looked over at Perry and he was looking pitiful.

"Yo', nigga, you gotta calm your little ass down. You've been a firecracker lately. And what the hell made you tell that man you fucked her the first night so you didn't know if she was special or not? Nigga, you wild for that," I said with a chuckle. "But baby girl put some fire to that face. I bet you won't say no shit like that again," I teased.

"Nigga, my face still fucking burning," Perry stated while shaking his head. About ten minutes later, Goddess and Journey finally came out but neither of them looked too happy.

"Baby, you good?" I asked.

"Yeah, I'm just hungry, that's all."

"Well, let's go get something to eat. Are y'all coming?" I asked Perry and Journey.

"Yeah, we coming," Perry answered for the both of them.

"Oh, you sure you want to go to dinner with someone who gave up the pussy on the first night?" Journey snapped.

"Damn babe, I didn't mean it like that, I swear. I shouldn't have said no stupid shit like that, especially to your father. I'm really sorry that I came off like that, ma. I'll never disrespect you like that again, ma, I swear."

Goddess and I excused ourselves to give them some privacy. The one thing I didn't do was involve myself in other people's love life, not even my brother's. Because I damn sure don't want nobody in my business. We finally got to Longhorn and I couldn't wait to eat because a nigga was hungry as shit. Those two finally got their shit together and we were able to enjoy our meals and we even had a drink before heading out. For some reason, I didn't want to be alone tonight so I asked Goddess to spend the night with me. Spending the night with her was the one thing that I have avoided because I wasn't sure if I would be able to refrain from putting this pipe in her. Goddess looked too good to lie next to me all night without hitting it. When we got to my house, we both showered and climbed into my king size bed. Just like I thought, my hands began to roam over her body as I thought about what her pops said about if I can't protect her leave her and there was no way I could. So, I knew I had to hire security for her and Journey as well.

I had my eyes closed as my hands and mind ran wild. When I opened my eyes, Goddess was staring at me and it felt like my soul had connected with hers. The feeling scared me just a little bit because it was something I haven't experienced before. I leaned in and kissed her soft lips and she deepened it. The way the kiss was going, I knew tonight was gonna be the night. My hand found its way between her thighs. I began to slowly rub on her swollen love button. Goddess moaned lightly in my ear. I inserted two fingers into her tight wetness and while rubbing her clit in a circular motion, I felt her muscles tightening up, but I wasn't ready for her to cum just yet. I pulled my fingers out then put them in my mouth. I kissed her lips once more before diving under the covers. I was ready to taste every drop of her nectar. I licked her swollen clit slowly in a circular motion. Her body started to squirm and she tried to pull away from my mouth and I grabbed her back into my mouth this time licking a little faster. I sucked her clit gently as inserted two fingers inside of her.

"Oh God, Princeton, you gonna make me cum," she cooed.

"That's what I want you to do. I want you to cum in my mouth." I licked, sucked, and fingered her wetness until her body was trembling and shaking hard.

"Fuck, Princeton! This shit feels so good! I'm about to cum!" Goddess moaned in the sexiest voice I've ever heard. After letting her juices run freely in my mouth, I made sure that I drunk every drop. I climbed in between her legs and kissed her passionately. Goddess was still trying to come down off the nut I just gave her. I freed her breast and started sucking on her nipples. Her moans had my dick super hard and I couldn't wait to feel her insides. I went to grab a condom but against my better judgment, I decided not to. I leaned down in her ear.

"Baby, are you on birth control?" I whispered. Goddess shook her head no and I contemplated if I should go ahead and grab one. "I want to feel you so I'm not going to wear a condom. I'm just gonna pull out." She looked hesitant for a second, but I eased into her not leaving her a chance to object.

"Shit," I groaned as I tried to fit my thickness into her walls. Goddess bit down on her bottom lip and that shit turned me on. Once I was finally in, I stroked in and out of her at a slow pace. Once Goddess was adjusted to my size, she started stroking me back from the bottom and that shit had a nigga on edge. "Shit Goddess, you feel so fucking good," I grunted as I pumped in and out of her. She was matching my every stroke and it made me wonder what her ride game was like and I was about to find out.

I flipped Goddess on top of me while still being inside of her. Once she found her rhythm, it was a wrap. I laid there and let her take me for the ride of my life. I swear it felt like I was in the softest place on earth. Goddess was riding my dick just right; not too fast and not too slow. Her perky breasts bounced up and down as she rode me. She was rocking her hips back and forth and side to side. I knew it wouldn't be much longer before I bust, but I wanted to enjoy her wetness just a little while longer. I shifted up just enough to put her breast in my mouth and that seemed to drive her crazy. Goddess placed her hands on my chest and sped up her strokes. I started stroking her from the bottom and felt myself about to cum.

"Ahhhh! Ahhhh! Oh God, Princeton, I'm about to cum, baby," she moaned loudly.

"Shit girl, me too," I told her as we climaxed together. I came so hard that I thought I lost part of my soul. We were both so into one another that we forgot that I wasn't wearing protection and she wasn't on the pill. But that shit was too good to pull out. What I did know was she was gonna have to get the on the pill or something because she was gonna be having my baby and soon with pussy that good. Goddess laid her head on my chest while I was still inside of her. I felt wetness on my chest but thought it was sweat until I heard her sniffle.

"Baby, what's wrong?" I asked lifting her head up. "Why are you crying?"

"I don't know. That shit just felt so good and my body never felt like that before," she told me. I wasn't quite sure how to respond since I was feeling the same way. I just wasn't about to cry but that shit was most definitely different from any woman I've ever been with.

"I know, ma. I feel the same way but don't cry because you're gonna feel like this every time I'm inside of you," I told her. The room fell silent for a moment as my raw emotions ran wild. Laying there had me feeling soft and I wasn't familiar with that. Which only meant one thing; I must be in love. I needed to talk to my mother about what I was feeling to make sure what I was feeling was real.

Goddess slept peacefully on my chest like this was her favorite spot to be and I was enjoying every moment of it. I found myself placing small kisses on her forehead as she slept. Yeah, I had to be in love doing this type of shit.

CHAPTER 7

Goddess

Tuesday morning

I walked into CVS Pharmacy and headed straight to the back where they kept the plan B pills because I couldn't afford to get pregnant right now. Last night had my mind blown because no one has ever made my body feel like that before. Although we've only been dating for a few months, I felt like I was in love with Princeton but my dad had me second-guessing my decision on being with him. My dad didn't knock what Princeton and Perry did for a living but it just didn't want that life for his girls and I understood that clearly. My sister could've been killed yesterday so I understand why my dad feels the way he does. After getting my Plan B, I headed to work. When I got there, I had an emergency that I needed to take care of. The entire time all I could do was think about the night I shared with Princeton. Of course, I was far from a virgin but the way he made me feel last night had me feeling like that was my very first time. That nigga had me crying and shit. I was feeling like a little girl. I knew that I love him but didn't want to say it first and be looking all crazy. These were the times I wished I had my mother or even a mother figure to talk to about these kinds of things. My dad did a great job and he's all I know, but I sometimes just want a woman's point of view on things but for now, I'll just have to vent and talk to Journey and Latrice as I always have. I noticed that Samantha hasn't been coming into my office as she usually does and I hoped that she was okay because that was unusual.

I was online looking up buildings. I decided that I was ready to work for myself as a therapist for families and children. Hopefully, I would only be here another month or so. I had an appointment after work to see about a building on Market Street. If it checks out to be what they say it is, I'm gonna go with it because I love the area and how the building looked. My phone buzzed indicating that I had a message.

Princeton: Hey baby, I can't seem to get you off my mind this morning. Last night was everything. Ain't gonna lie, you got a nigga hooked and I hope you know I was serious when I told you once I put this dick in you that the pussy belongs to me forever.

I was blushing from ear to ear reading his text. I didn't know why women liked when a nigga told us our pussy was theirs. I guess its confirmation that it was good.

Me: Hey baby, I've been thinking about you all morning as well. I hope you know the same rules apply to you. That's my dick and my dick only.

Him: After being inside of you last night, you don't have to worry about me fucking around with no low-grade pussy when yours is laced in gold.

I cracked up laughing because that was the first time I heard some shit like that but anything was possible with these niggas.

Me: You sure do have a way with words, but I love it. I would like to see you tonight but it has to be after I go look at the building I was telling you about.

Princeton: Cool, that sounds good. I'll see you tonight.

Later that evening

As soon as I clocked out, I headed out so I could go look at the building. I got there in ten minutes and just as I thought it was perfect, I had so many ideas on what I wanted to do with my office. It was spacious with a lot of potential. After looking at every room again I was sold.

"I love this place, so I would like to purchase this building," I told the owner.

"I'm glad to hear that. All you have to do is fill out a few papers and the place is yours," she stated.

"Well, let's get started," I told her. After filling out all the paper, she handed me a copy of the thing that I signed. I pulled out my checkbook to seal the deal.

"You are aware that this building has already been paid for?" I looked at her like she was crazy because how could I have paid for something that I wasn't even sure I was even buying?

"There must be some kind of mistake. I haven't paid for anything yet."

"I'll be right back. Let me go retrieve the paperwork," she told me before getting up from the desk. I wasn't worried about her damn paperwork because I knew I didn't pay for anything. I sat there patiently waiting for her to return as my mind drifted off to the night I shared with Princeton. A couple of minutes later the door opened and when I looked up, Princeton was standing there with some roses and a big ass grin.

"Oh my God, what are you doing here?"

"I just wanted to be here to see your face when they tell you that your very first business has been paid in full by the greatest boyfriend ever."

"Princeton, you didn't?" I squealed.

"I sure did. I knew how much you liked this building and was pretty sure you would want it so I brought it for you. And you already know that everything is in your name. Now, let's get out of here so we can celebrate," he said, picking me up and spinning me around like I was a skinny girl. I placed a kiss on his lips.

"Oh my God, Princeton, thank you! I love you so much," I blurted not believing how easily the words escaped from my lips.

"I love you, too, Goddess," he replied kissing me in the mouth like it was just the two of us. "I'm gonna show you just how much I love your ass as soon as I get you alone tonight." I was so happy that I didn't know what to do with myself. After I got my keys to my new building, we headed out the door.

Princeton had me drive my car to his place then hopped in his so we could go to dinner. We decided to go to Red Lobster tonight. After being seated, we ordered our food and drinks. I was so in tuned with what Princeton was saying until I heard a familiar voice.

"So, you really fucking with this thug over me?" Aaron questioned.

"I think you need to watch your mouth and how you speak to my woman," Princeton chimed in.

"I don't recall talking to you. I was talking to Goddess," Aaron barked.

"Yo', I know your feelings is hurt that I took your girl but this is my only warning. You need to get the fuck away from my table with that bullshit before it becomes a problem," Princeton warned in a serious tone.

"Aaron, I think you should leave. This isn't the time or the place to have this conversation," I stated trying to defuse the situation.

"Man, fuck you and that pussy ass nigga you with," were the last words spoken before Princeton punched Aaron in his mouth. They started fighting and it was gonna take an army to break them up. I tried to pull Princeton off of Aaron before he killed him but he was too strong for me. The fight finally came to an end and Aaron looked pretty bad. His face was leaking blood and his eyes looked damn near shut.

"Let's get the fuck outta here before I end up behind bars tonight," Princeton said throwing money on the table for the bill.

"Oh my God baby, what happened to you?" I heard a female's voice say to Aaron. When I looked up, I locked eyes with my coworker Samantha. To say I was shocked would be an understatement.

"Really Samantha? Wow, that's fucked up," was all I could say to her before walking out of the restaurant. I had so many different emotions flowing through my body. I knew I moved on and all but that was fucked and sheisty as hell. Like, Samantha was really fucking with my ex. That explains why she hasn't been in my office; she was avoiding me. We were definitely gonna have words but tonight wasn't the night; it was enough going on. When we got in the car, Princeton told his driver Mark what took place in the restaurant then rest of the ride was silent. I wasn't sure what to say to him because I've never seen him this mad before and I didn't want to say the wrong shit to make matters worse. When we got in the house, as soon as the door shut, it was like nothing ever happened.

"Take your clothes off. Every damn piece," he demanded. I did as I was told. I stood in front of him ass naked as the day I was born. Princeton sat on the couch admiring my body from head to toe. It felt like he was looking through my soul. I have never had a man that looked at me that way. After two hours of great love making and fucking, we finally took our asses to sleep.

When I woke up the next morning, all I could think about was what took place last night. I knew Aaron felt some type of way about what happened between us but he was in rare form last night. I got up and dressed for work trying not to wake up Princeton but when I walked into the room, he was already waked.

"Good morning, beautiful. Did you sleep okay?" Princeton asked me.

"Yes, I slept great thanks to you," I answered in a flirty tone.

"If you want to make it to work today, I would strongly suggest you cut that flirty shit out," he replied seriously. As much as I would have loved to stay at home with him and have him inside of me, I just couldn't do that today, so I kept my mouth closed.

"Well, I guess I better keep quiet because I have to work today," I told him.

"I guess you better but listen, you need to go get on birth control like yesterday because you gonna get pregnant." I thought about what he said and made a mental note to buy another Plan B if wasn't too late. I was gonna call and make an appointment when I went on break this afternoon.

"Also, I hired you a new driver named Bones. He'll be taking you everywhere you need to go until I get some shit handled."

I wasn't sure what this was about or how I felt about it, but I know that day at my father's house he told Journey and I not to ask any questions. He told us to just listen and watch our surroundings at all times. I didn't bother to say anything. I just gathered my belongings and kissed Princeton on the lips before leaving out the door.

When I got to the door, Bones didn't look shit like his name. They should call that nigga Muscle or Body, some shit like that. He was actually really nice looking with a body out this world.

"Good morning, Ms. Jenkins," he greeted while opening my door.

"Good morning," I spoke back. I got in the car feeling a tad bit weird. The ride was silent so I decided to spark up a conversation. "How are you this morning?"

"I'm well but with all due respect, I was told not to engage in any type of personal conversation. Only hi and bye and that's about it. Orders from the boss."

For some reason, that infuriated me. That sounded like some crazy shit if you ask me. I snatched up the phone and called Princeton.

"Is everything okay, baby?" he answered on the first ring.

"How dare you hire me a driver then tell him not to speak to me outside of hi or bye? You don't control me, Princeton. You don't get to tell me who to talk to," I yelled. The line was silent for a moment before he spoke.

"We'll deal with that shit later," he spoke angrily. I went to speak but realized the line went dead. "I know damn well that nigga didn't hang up on me," I mumbled. At this point, my blood was boiling. He had a lot of fucking nerve. When we pulled up at my job, I got out the car without saying a word. I walked into my office and closed the door. Minutes later, there was a tap on the door.

"Goddess, can we talk?" Samantha thirsty ass had the nerve to ask.

"Now you wanna talk, Samantha? How dare your thirsty ass date my ex after I was just with him a few months ago? I wish y'all the best but do me a favor and stay the fuck away from me. If it's not work-related, don't say shit to me," I spat.

"Goddess, I'm sorry. I never meant for things to turn out this way." I gave her a death stare and the bitch was still standing in my office.

"Can you please leave my office, Samantha? I don't want to talk to you," I stated harshly. I guess she finally got the message because she left without another word. My workday seemed long and I was ready to get the hell up out of there. Tonight was the night I was having dinner with my dad and my sister and I couldn't wait because I needed to vent.

Later that night

I walked out of work but didn't see the car outside. Just as I reached for my phone, I felt someone grab me from behind by my mouth and then everything went black. When I woke up, I was in a dark room tied up. I couldn't believe someone had kidnapped me. I looked around and no one was in the room. I was scared as shit. I had to pee bad as hell. "Her hoe ass should be up by now," I heard a voice say. I tried to listen hard but I couldn't make out the voice. I heard footsteps coming down the basement then the door opened.

"Damn, I can see why he's tripping over her," I heard the guy mumble. "Yo' boss, she's up!" he yelled. Another set of footsteps came down the steps and I couldn't believe my fucking eyes when they landed on Aaron. This nigga had to have lost his fucking mind. Suddenly, I wasn't scared anymore; I was actually entertained.

"Where your bitch ass nigga at now?" he asked cockily, snatching the tape from my mouth.

"Really Aaron? You really fucking kidnaped me? What do think is gonna happen or do you plan to kill me?" I asked rolling my eyes.

"If I don't get my fucking ten million dollars you're a dead woman. Let's see how much your punk ass boyfriend really care," Aaron barked and I don't know what it was about his statement, but I started laughing so fucking hard that I damn near pissed myself. "What the fuck is funny?" he snapped.

"You're what's funny, Aaron," I told him while laughing harder than before.

"You stuck up bitch," he yelled while smacking me so hard, that me and the chair hit the floor.

"Yo, what the fuck you doing? You said we weren't gonna hurt her," the other guy asked.

"Fuck that! I'm about to fuck her up then fuck the shit out of her since she thinks shit funny."

My heart started beating fast at the thought of Aaron raping me. Hell, I didn't want to be beaten either, but I rather him hit me then to stick his dick in me again. I wasn't worried about not making it out of here because I knew if no one else, my daddy was coming to get me and Aaron would be dead by the end of the night. I just hoped he got here before he violated me. I would have never thought for a second that he was capable of no shit like that but he did kidnap me then hit me and he planned to ask for ten million dollars. It didn't take a rocket scientist to know he didn't think this shit through and forgot who my father was and he damn sure didn't do his research on my boyfriend.

"Man, you crazy as hell. That shit wasn't part of the plan. Ain't nobody say shit about rape and beating no woman. You tripping now, Aaron," the dude said. Aaron pulled out a gun and pointed it at the guy.

"Nigga, I know you not bitching out on me cause I'll kill you right here and now," Aaron said pointing the gun at the guy. Now I was really scared because this nigga done went crazy.

"Man, chill and get that fucking gun out of my face." Aaron stood there for a few still pointing the gun. He finally put it down and the guy looked relieved. The room was silent for a few minutes at first. "Yo', go upstairs and give me some privacy while I deep stroke that pussy," Aaron stated.

"Aaron, please don't rape me, please," I begged. He laughed at me then walked towards me and started stroking my hair. My stomach felt sick and I felt like I was about to throw up. And that's just what I attended to do and piss myself too if that would keep his dick out of me.

"There's nothing you can say to stop me from putting this dick in you. We gonna see who has the last laugh," he stated laughing hard as hell. Aaron grabbed my breasts and I threw up every fucking where. Aaron got so mad with me he hit me again and again until I played like I was unconscious and fell back on the floor. After hitting the floor, everything seemed to go black. I could hear but I couldn't open my eyes.

Rashaad

"Journey, where the hell is your sister? This isn't like her to be late for our dinners. Well, not this late especially without calling or texting."

"Dad, I don't know. I called her phone but her voicemail came right on," Journey answered. Just as I pulled out my phone to call her myself my phone rang. It wasn't a number I was familiar with so I answered on the first ring.

"Hello, who's this?"

"It's Princeton. Have you seen Goddess?" he replied.

"Nah, she didn't show up to dinner and her phone is going straight to voice mail."

"Fuck!" he yelled. "Something is wrong. I came to pick her up but she's not there and not answering. This can't be good, I think someone took her," Princeton yelled into the phone. I felt the blood drain from my body after hearing him say that. I didn't know who the hell had my baby but what I did know was I was gonna find her and this would be their last day breathing.

"What the fuck you mean you think someone has her?" I yelled not giving a damn that I was in a restaurant. The line went silent and that pissed me off, but I had to find my daughter so I didn't have time to sit on the phone with him being angry. "Listen, I have a tracker on her so I know how to find her, but I have to hang up when I track the address. I'll send it to you so you can meet me over there," I told him before hanging up. When I hung up the phone, Journey had tracked her down from her iPhone. I knew then the person who took Goddess was amateur. I shot Princeton the address then headed over there. Whoever had Goddess was right in Camden not too far from her job. She was right in Parkside. It took me ten minutes to get to my destination. When I pulled up, Princeton was already there. I pulled my gun from my secret compartment in the car and got out. Princeton and Perry and a few other dudes were there as well. We parked a few blocks over in the back of the house.

We walked up to the door and I kicked that shit in. I didn't have time to play around with these niggas. When we got in the house, it looked like it belonged to a woman. No one was in the living room or any of the bedrooms. I walked in the kitchen and heard noises in the basement so I knew that's where my daughter was being held. I ran down the stairs and the sight before me caused me to lose it. I put a bullet into a nigga's head that was standing there while Princeton was beating the shit of the man that looked like he was about to rape my daughter. I joined Princeton with the ass whooping. I drew my gun when I realized it was Aaron.

"Let me do it, daddy. I want to kill him," Goddess said barely above a whisper catching me and Princeton's attention at the same time. I past her my gun and watched my baby girl shoot that nigga in the head, splitting his head in half. The shocked looked on Princeton's face when I saw my baby handle that gun like she did had me tickled a little bit. We heard another sound coming from upstairs and a woman was walking down the stairs calling for Aaron. No sooner then she got down the steps her body dropped and hit the floor as blood oozed from her head.

"Oh my God, that's Samantha," Goddess said while shaking her head. We all headed out the same way we entered. The cleanup crew came just to make sure there were no signs of my daughter was ever there.

I was relieved to have my daughter back, but I wasn't too happy with the sight of her. She looked as if she had pissed and thrown up on herself. I watched as Princeton catered to Goddess, I could tell that he was in love with her. I needed to know how the hell she ended up by herself when I wanted detail on her at all times. Once we got to my house, Goddess went upstairs to shower and when she came back down, I needed to know how the fuck this happened.

"I thought I told you that I didn't want my fucking daughter by herself until y'all got rid of that nigga?" I barked, looking Princeton dead in his eyes. He held up his hands in the surrender position before speaking.

"Look, I don't know how this shit happened. I had her driver drop her off this morning, but I was gonna pick her up when she got off. I called her a few times and she didn't answer so I texted her that I would be the one picking her up and not to leave the building until I got there. So unless she got kidnapped in a building full of people, then that means her ass didn't listen," Princton stated angrily. "So, what the fuck happened, Goddess? How the fuck did your ex kidnapped you?" She put her head down before answering his question.

"I never read your text because I was mad at you. I went outside thinking that Bones was out there then someone came up from behind me and put something on my mouth and I passed out. When I woke up, I was tied up in a basement. Long story short, Aaron planned to call and ask for a ten-million-dollar ransom from Princeton and when I started laughing, he hit me then said he was gonna rape me. The thought of him raping made me sick to my stomach so I threw up then I decided to piss myself to make myself less desirable but all that did was piss him off even more. Things seemed to go black then shortly after y'all came. I knew y'all would find me. I just hoped that y'all made it before he raped me," Goddess cried.

I was so hurt and so angry but I didn't know who the hell to be angry with more. I liked these guys as people but I honestly didn't like them as much for my daughter's. My girls were everything to me and I seemed to be losing them to these guys that they've only known for a short period. My daughters were prepared for danger and could handle themselves but never needed to because I made sure to keep them out of harm's way.

"Goddess, I'm sorry about what happened to you today but you caused this shit on yourself in some way or another. First you sneaking off acting like a little hoe with his ass in the bathroom getting your pussy ate while you're at an event with your boyfriend. You should've never entertained this man while you were with Aaron. What did you think was gonna happen? That nigga felt played. That didn't give him a right to do what he did today but love make you do some crazy shit. Then you choose to date a street nigga and now you gotta watch your back when they have beef because y'all are just as much as a target as they are. I sat both of you down and told you what your life would be while dealing with them but neither of you listened. I told y'all what was expected from y'all as a street legend's woman and you didn't listen to that either and because you were mad, you didn't answer your fucking phone!" I yelled. The tears were rolling down her cheeks and at that time, I could care less. I was in rare form and I was gonna say what I needed to say on this day then be over with it. I didn't have time to pacify no grown folk feelings. "I have news for you, honey. Being mad at him doesn't change the rules of the game and keep your ass out of danger, but I guess you can see that now?" I asked sarcastically.

"Daddy, she's been through enough. Do you have to do this tonight?" Journey asked laced with hurt.

"You fucking right I have to do this today because y'all seem to continue to do stupid shit that you didn't do before but I'm about to let y'all be grown and do what y'all want. I've taught y'all all I could now it's time for me to let y'all live. Both of y'all have disappointed me badly over the last few months. I tried to stay out of and mind my business but y'all don't want to listen. And as far as y'all go," I said, pointing to Princeton and Perry. "If y'all gonna be with my daughters, I suggest you protect them better and put them in check. Because for some supposed to be street legends, y'all fucking up. I'm so pissed and hurt right now that I don't think I should say anything else. Y'all free to leave. Girls, I love y'all with everything in me. I'll probably reach out in a few days. I need a mental break. Y'all can let yourselves out," I told them then left out the living room and went into my den. I needed a drink.

I knew I hurt my girls feelings and had them wondering what had gotten into me, but I couldn't deal with that at the moment. It was just something that I felt like they needed to hear. After a few drinks and smoking two blunts, I finally took my ass to sleep. I didn't even bother to eat anything. I just wanted for the night to be over. I would deal with everything else at another time.

Princeton

I was so pissed at myself for what I allowed to happen today, I was starting to wonder if I should continue to be in a relationship with Goddess. She was everything that a man could dream of having and I couldn't even keep her safe from a regular nigga that wasn't even about the street life so how could I protect her if something major was gonna happened? I wasn't used to dealing with someone like her. Rashaad was right; the only person I really ever had to protect was my myself and Perry and now we were both with two beautiful woman that deserved the world. They shouldn't have to watch their backs or have security with them at all times. That's not really a good way to live and it took being with Goddess to learn that. She was staying with her sister tonight because she was really fucked up over everything that happened today and the shit her father said to her really fucked her up. I put someone to stay over there with them tonight to make sure they were good.

Rashaad had got back to me and my brother about that Tommy guy and first thing in the morning, I planned to go take care of his ass. I didn't play about my fucking money. Rashaad was able to find out that he had it out for me and my brother over some beef he had with my dad. Apparently, he had some type of crush on my momma but she chose my dad. What the fuck that had to do with us damn near thirty years later, but I was about to find out. I didn't have time to deal with petty shit that didn't have shit to do with me. My pops have been dead for years now. Besides, that was their beef. That shit didn't have anything to do with me and my brother.

The next morning

When I woke the next morning, I showered and threw on some sweatpants and a tee with a pair of Air Max. We had to be at the airport in an hour to Michigan. I already had a few men there watching Tommy's every move for the last week. They said he didn't seem like he had much of a life but he definitely seemed like a wannabe nigga. When I got to the airport Perry was already there. Our flight took off soon after. Damn near six hours later we arrived in Michigan. We went straight to the car rental to get a car. When we left there, we headed to our hotel room. I was starving so I was just gonna order room service.

"Yo', I been thinking about leaving the game," I told Perry. He just looked over at me before saying anything.

"Yeah, me too, Bro. I mean, we do have more money than we can spend in this lifetime," Perry replied.

"We sure do, plus, I'm ready to settle down and have some kids and I can't be looking over my shoulders. We never really had anybody come for us until now and although we can hold our own, this isn't what I want to do for the rest of my life, you feel me?"

"I've been thinking about the same shit. I just didn't want to get out the game and leave you hanging cause you already know; we ride together, we die together," Perry stated passing me the blunt to hit.

"Hell yeah. Well, let's handle this nigga first then we can talk about this shit later. A nigga hungry and tired as hell right now," I told him passing the blunt back to him. When we got to the hotel, we went into our rooms which were right next door to each other with adjoining doors. I ordered room service then got in the shower. After eating, I decided to give Goddess a call but she didn't answer the phone. I guess she was still in her feelings and wanted to be left alone because she didn't answer. I smoked another blunt then took my ass to sleep.

Later that night

A few hours later, I woke up from my nap ready to go see what was up with this clown ass nigga. I tapped on Perry's door and when he answered, he was already fully dressed and ready. That's why I fucked with my brother the long way because he was always ready and down for whatever I was ready for.

"Damn, pretty boy. I thought we were about to go kill a nigga and you dressed like you about to go fuck a bitch," I told him and we both laughed.

"Nigga, you dumb as hell for that one. You a straight clown. Is your ass ready to go handle this nigga or what?"

"Nigga, I'll be ready in 20 minutes," I told him closing my door. I looked down at my phone and saw that Goddess had called me back so I called her.

"Hello?" she answered in a low tone.

"Hey baby, how you feeling? I miss you already," I told her.

"I'm a little better. I'm just mentally fucked up about everything that took place yesterday with Aaron and then my dad. This shit is crazy. I never saw my life being like this," Goddess said sadly.

"Yeah, I know baby. Listen, when I get back tomorrow, we need to talk, but I gotta go. I have to take care of something. I love you, Goddess. Be safe and get better. And if you need me, call me. I don't care what time it is."

"I love you, too, Princeton." It was something about the way she told me she love me that sent chills down my spine. When I hung up the phone, Perry ass was standing in the doorway smiling and shit.

"Nigga, what the fuck you standing in my door smiling for?"

"I'm smiling at your pussy whipped ass. You must have finally hit that. That's why your ass been acting all crazy and shit over her lately. I ain't never heard you tell no female that you love outside of momma."

"Nigga, shut your nosey ass up and the next female you hear me say that shit to will be my daughter now let's get outta here," I told him making sure I had all my shit before walking out the door. When we got in the car, I hit my homie up and he said this was the perfect time to come cause the nigga was there alone. He already scoped the place out so we knew exactly how to get in and all that. My homie even had cameras set in his house so he would be able to see and hear everything that nigga was doing.

We pulled around back like we were told to do. I made sure my silencer was on and I had my other shit ready before walking up to the house. I stuck a card between the lock to get in. This shit was too easy. Nobody was downstairs so we went up. The closer we got I could have sworn I heard grunting from a man and became pissed cause I was told he was here alone. Oh well, I was here now. I opened the door with ease and this nigga was watching porn with his eyes closed beating the shit out of his dick. I just shook my head before walking in the room.

"Well, look who's beating their little dick," Perry said causing me to laugh at his stupid ass.

"What the fuck!" Tommy said while jumping up with his dick in his hand but with two guns pointed at him, he froze right where he stood. We had literally caught this nigga with his dick in his hand. I don't know why but I thought this shit was actually funny.

"Why did you come for us and cut the shit, you might as well tell the truth because I have no intentions on letting you live."

"Wow, if it isn't Princeton in the flesh", Tommy said with a smile and I was ready to just kill him and get it over with.

"Nigga, shut the fuck up with the small talk. Why did you come for me and my brother over some beef you had with my pops years ago. That's some bitch nigga shit," I barked.

"That's just it, Princeton. You have every fucking thing to with it. Since I'm gonna die anyway, the least I can do is tell you the truth. That nigga you call pops took my family and for the record, you're my fucking son not his," he blurted.

"Nigga, I'll blow your fucking head off if you ever say some stupid shit like that again," I blurted, ready to kill this nigga cause now he was just making up shit.

"I don't have to lie and I have proof. Your momma and I was fucking around before her and Charlie but no one really knew but a few people including Charlie, but I guess his money was longer than mine and he had more swag because he managed to start fucking her. I put two and two together cause she started acting funny and didn't want to fuck around anymore. Then one night, we were all hanging out and Charlie was all over her ass. I mean, kissing her in the mouth and all. I became so enraged that night that him and I got into a fight because I didn't understand how he could stab me in the back like that. Anyway, long story short, she found out she was pregnant and said it was Charlie's kid, but I knew deep down you were mine. Anyway, she used to hang with my sister so after you were born, I had my sister swab you when she was babysitting and sure enough, you were mine like I thought. I still have the fucking paperwork. Anyway, I took the papers to your momma and she had a fit that I knew the truth and begged me not to tell Charlie but she had me fucked up if she thought I was gonna let another nigga raise my fucking son. Soon after, my sister went missing and till this day, she's never been seen again and I knew your momma and Charlie was the reason. He put out a million-dollar hit on my head so I had to lay low. When least expected, I popped back up long enough to catch that nigga slipping. I murked his ass so quick. He took the three things that matter the most to me; you, my sister, and your momma. So, I had taken his life. The papers are under the bed in a box. I never planned for you to get hurt, but I realized after the attack, I was being foolish. That's why I stopped. But if you gonna kill me then just do it, I don't have shit to live for now anyway." After hearing him talk, for some reason, I knew he wasn't lying and I halfway felt sorry for him. But I knew I couldn't let him live. And even though I didn't have a relationship with this man or even know him for that matter, if what he said was true, I couldn't pull the trigger on my own flesh and blood so I would have to let Perry do it for me.

I wasn't quite sure why the fuck I was having a hard time with not wanting to kill him because normally, he would've been dead a few sentences in. I held the gun on him and told Perry to get the box. I needed to verify what he said. He pulled out the box and passed it to me. I rummaged through the papers until I found what I was looking for. And sure enough, I was this nigga's son. My eyes filled with tears and I wasn't sure why. I had so much emotion towards this.

"Is it true, bro?" Perry asked, breaking me from my thoughts. I just nodded my head. "Damn," he mumbled.

"Put the gun down and let's go," I told him. They both looked at me like I was crazy.

"Nigga, what you mean?" Perry asked.

"Just what I said, let's go. I'm gonna let you live, but I'm taking these papers. Don't make me regret this," I told him before walking out of the room with a confused Perry behind me.

"Yo', man, what the fuck was that about? I know damn well you not about to let that nigga live because he supposed to be your pops?" Perry asked, but I didn't feel like talking about the shit so I just ignored his ass. I really had to gather my thoughts about this shit. The one thing that I knew was I was on the next flight to Atlanta to pay my mom a visit because she was gonna explain this shit to me. When we made it back to the car, I just sat there in a daze for a few trying processes what I just heard and saw on that paperwork. I guess Perry got the point and stopped questioning me. He sat there quiet and rolled a blunt. I pulled out the paperwork and read that shit three more times before finally putting it away. Perry passed me the blunt and I hit that shit long and hard, but I knew I was gonna need another one right after this. Three blunts later, I was high as shit.

"Yo', I can't believe this shit, yo'. You know we about to go visit your momma and I'm not sure how it's gonna go. This shit got me fucked up badly, bro. This is too much to take in but right now, I need to eat then look up flights. I'm not even telling her that I coming."

"Yeah, this shit is crazy, but I can't believe you let that nigga walk even after admitting to killing pops. I don't know if I could let that shit fly, bro. I'm not even gonna hold you."

"Look, we not touching him unless I say so. Just chill on that for right now." The car went silent but I could tell that he didn't like what I said, but I wasn't beat to deal with his shit right now. We pulled up at some wing spot. When we walked in, we were seated. I ordered myself thirty wings and some fries, that's how hungry I was.

Once we got our food and ate, I was ready to go back to the room. I needed some alone time to clear my head. Perry and I didn't say anything to one another the entire ride and I was cool with that. When I got back to the room, I booked a 9 a.m. flight and I shot Perry the information then laid my ass down to go to sleep. I was still high and full so what the combination of the two it put me out like a light. My phone ringing over and over again caused me to jump up. When I looked at the phone it was Goddess. I snatched it up thinking it was an emergency.

"Hello?" I answered groggily.

"Baby, you sleep?" she said sounding like she was crying.

"Yeah, I was sleep, but baby, what's wrong? Why are you crying, baby?"

"I just can't stop thinking about what happened last night and then with my dad laying into me the way he did really got me messed up in the head. I just wish you were here with me," she cried.

"I know baby and we will deal with that when I get back. I just had some crazy shit pop off out here my damn self so we both have plenty to talk about. But just try to get some sleep. I might be back tomorrow depending on how shit plays out at my mom's. Get some rest. I love you more than you know. If you want, we can sleep on the phone together," I offered

"I love you, too, Princeton and yes, it would make me feel so much better knowing that you're on the phone."

"Aight, let's go to sleep."

The next morning when I woke up, Goddess was still on the phone sleeping. Her light breathing in my ear caused me to smile. I wasn't sure if I should just hang up or wake her up to let her know that I was hanging up. I decided to just hang up because I didn't want to interrupt the only sleep she'd probably gotten. I didn't even bother to shower. I was just ready to go confront my mother, even though I had no clue where to begin or how to even approach it. A knock on my door broke me from my thoughts. I already knew it was my brother so I opened it.

"Yo' bro, I just wanted to say sorry about last night. I was being insensitive to your feelings. That was some deep shit to take in so I don't blame you for what you did. I probably would have done the same thing," he stated.

"Thanks, bro. I appreciated that. Let's roll out and get this over with," I told him while heading out the door.

Later that night

When I got to my mom's house, she was cooking dinner. She was shocked beyond words to see us.

"Oh my God, my babies are here! What a surprise," she said, hugging and kissing both of us on the cheek. When she pulled back from our hug, I couldn't help but admire her beauty. My mom was 5'5 with the body of a twenty-year-old. She was light-skinned with dark red hair. She didn't dress, look, or act like a fifty-year-old woman.

"Mom, I came to talk to you about something," I told her getting straight to the point.

"Well, it must be pretty important if y'all flew all the way here just to talk so let's talk," she replied.

"Who's Tommy?" The look on her face was priceless. She looked like a deer caught in headlights.

"Someone I knew from back in the day. What is this about?"

"Look, I don't feel like playing any games or beating around the bush. Is that nigga my pops?" I blurted.

"Why the hell would you ask some stupid shit like that? Princeton, you know damn well who your father is. I can't believe the nerve of you," she snapped like her lying ass was telling the truth.

"I never thought I'll see the day that you would stand in my face and tell me a bald-faced lie like that. So, if he's not my father then why the fuck do I have paperwork stating that he is?" I yelled angrily. I really hoped that she would have told me the truth the first time.

Whap! She smacked the shit out of me so hard and fast, that I didn't even see that shit coming. I swear if she wasn't my momma, I would have smacked the fuck out of her. A part of me still wanted to.

"I don't give a damn how mad you are. If you ever speak to me like that again, I'll put a bullet in you myself!" she yelled. I stood there biting the inside of my jaw. That's how pissed I was. My feelings being hurt and her lying to my face caused me to lash out in a way that I would never have thought about doing with my momma. And I didn't even care about the consequences.

"You smacked me because you're a fucking liar and I called you out on your bullshit? Hell, are you even my real fucking mom?" I barked as I felt the tears fall freely down my face. Here I was standing in my momma's kitchen cursing and crying like a damn fool. I was hurt and angry. I don't know why I was so pissed off, I just wanted answers. I loved my pops. He raised Perry and I to be the best men we could be, but I wondered how different my life would have been if I would have known my real father. How do you force a man out of his child's life? My mom was now crying and I somewhat felt bad. I'm sure she was hurt, disappointed, and embarrassed.

"Look, I'm gonna give you a pass this time cause I can clearly see that you're hurt or either lost your mind. But you're right, he is your father and the story is too long and probably wouldn't make any sense to tell it anyway. But what I will say is your father Charlie wasn't the man y'all thought he was especially in your younger days. He did some very ruthless things and because of the money and power he had, he was damn near untouchable. I was messing with Tommy first but your father wanted me so he took me himself. Soon after, I found out that I was pregnant and I knew that Tommy was the father but Charlie wasn't beat to hear it. So, he wanted to raise you for himself. Why, I don't know. Tommy had his sister swab you one day when she was babysitting you. Anyway, he fought hard to be in your life but Charlie wasn't having it so he put a hit out on him. I haven't seen or heard from Tommy since. I was young and dumb plus, your dad used to beat the shit out of me in the beginning of our relationship.

I used to be scared of your father. One day, he almost killed me and from that day, he never put his hands on me again and taught y'all the 'no woman no kids' rule but he didn't always live by that. I'm sorry for what I've done. I never meant to hurt you and I damn sure never thought you would find out. I don't really know what else to say. And if I'm assuming correctly, if you have papers, that means you've spoken to Tommy. I thought he was dead; how did he find you?" she asked.

"Long story. I can't believe this shit," I mumbled. "What happened to his sister? Is she dead?" I asked. My mom looked shocked that I knew about her.

"Your father paid her to disappear or die. Of course, she took the money and left and no one has heard from her again. I was so hurt because Tammy was one of my closet friends," my mom cried. Perry was just standing there looking just as lost and confused as I was. I couldn't even lie, all this shit was just too much to take in. I didn't know what to feel or how to feel.

"Well, because of you and dad's stupid decisions is the reason why your husband Charlie was killed. Yup, your ex-lover killed my fucking dad. And after hearing the entire story, I can't say that I blame him. This entire story sounds like some shit you watch in a movie and I don't care to hear anymore, I'm out," Perry blurted before exiting the kitchen. My mom tried calling after him but her calls fell on deaf ears. Nothing was said between the two of us for the first few seconds. I personally had no clue what to say or if I wanted to say anything else.

"Mom, how could you keep this from us after all of these years?"

"Honestly Princeton, after all this time and Charlie being dead already and me thinking that Tommy was dead; I just didn't feel like it was important anymore. Most of the time, I didn't even think about it. I was caught so off guard when you asked me that I just said the first thing that popped in my head. I'm sorry, Princeton. I never meant to hurt you or your brother. I know it's going to take a while to digest. But please forgive me. I was young and dumb."

"Did you love Tommy?" I asked not quite sure why.

"Honestly, I was in love with him. Sometimes, it feels like I still am. There are days I wished I didn't get involved with Charlie. Charlie just had more money and power than Tommy, but Tommy treated me better than any man ever had," my mom confessed. I was shocked as hell to learn that because my mother and father seemed to be so happy and like the perfect couple.

"I just need some time to deal with all of this. I didn't mean to disrespect you, but I was so angry and then the fact that you lied about it sent me off the edge. I'll be in touch but I really need to go because this is just too much. I'll call you in a few days once I clear my head. I have to find your other hot-headed son," I told her honestly.

"Princeton, I know you're upset but I want you to know that I truly am sorry for hurting you so badly. I love you, son." The room fell silent because I couldn't say the words back and it wasn't because I didn't love her. I just didn't want to say it right now. As soon as I got outside, I called Perry and he answered on the first ring.

"Yo', where you at?" I asked.

"I walked around the corner to the bar. Why? You ready to be out?"

"Yeah, I'm ready but I'll meet you at the bar. After this shit, I need a drink my damn self."

After a few drinks with my brother, I thought it wouldn't be such a bad idea to go back to Rashaad's club tonight to have some fun and clear our minds. We went and bought an outfit to wear tonight before finding a hotel to check into. Two hours later, we were sitting in VIP at the club popping bottles. We had a couple of females that were trying to chill with us, but I wasn't off that. Goddess was the only one for me. Plus, what I look like disrespecting her like that in her daddy's shit? I was feeling nice and thought my eyes were playing tricks on me when I thought I saw Rashaad at the bar being over-friendly with the bartender. But after doing a second look, I confirmed it indeed was him. I decided to go to the bar and say hello. Perry decided to stay behind and continue to drink plus, he wasn't a big fan of Rashaad. It was weird because he actually liked him but didn't like him. As far as myself, I liked him a lot and felt like I could learn a lot from him. I guess you can say I somewhat admired him. The love he showed for his daughters was like nothing I'd ever seen. I guess I have to have a child of my own to understand it.

"Hey Rashaad," I spoke.

"Hey, Princeton, wassup? What brings you here? You're the last person I expected to run into."

"Some crazy shit went down that I needed to handle. As a matter of fact, do you have a minute to go somewhere private and talk?" I asked.

"Sure, we can go up to my office. Shantae, excuse me for a moment. I shall return," he told the bartender before walking off. When we got up to his office, I was impressed. His shit looked like a mini living room. "So, what can I do for you, Princeton?" he asked, breaking me from my thoughts.

"Were you aware that Tommy is my real father?" I asked, getting straight to the point. He looked at me like I had three heads on my shoulders.

"Charlie is your father. Where the hell did you get that information from?"

"Well, when I went to go handle Tommy a couple of nights ago, he told me he was my father and showed me paperwork to prove it. That shit fucked me up so I went to my momma and she confirmed that the shit was true. So, I'm a little fucked up right now."

"Damn, that's fucked up. I never knew that shit. I know this is a lot to take in but everything is gonna be okay. Is Tommy still breathing?" he asked me with a smirk.

"Yeah, once that nigga showed me paperwork, I just couldn't off that nigga, not even after he admitted to killing Charlie. After hearing everything, I felt he did what he had to do. I'm hurt, mad, and confused but there are rules to the game and the shit that Charlie did, he definitely broke the rules. I just feel so bad for what my momma and daddy did to that man. I don't know how to feel. I just wanna get home to your daughter. She's really going through I right now we both are."

"Well, I'm sorry about all the shit you just found out but it'll work out. And as far as my daughter goes, she will be okay. I wouldn't be here if I thought she wouldn't be. I have eyes on her as well, since y'all don't like to listen. But let me get back out here and finish enjoying myself. I'm heading back home tomorrow."

"Aight well, thanks for the talk, I really appreciate."

"No problem, young blood. Enjoy the rest of your night. Where's your brother at?"

"He decided to stay in VIP."

"Yeah, I bet. I know that nigga don't care for me but hell if I care, I won't lose no sleep," Rashaad said with a chuckle. I just shook my head before walking out of his office.

The next morning

As soon as we got back home, the only thing I wanted to do was see my baby Goddess. I was missing her ass like crazy. I just wanted to hold her and feel the insides of those tight wet walls. I pulled up to her house and parked. When I got to the door, I heard the TV on. I knocked then heard her little footsteps walking towards the door.

"Who is it?" a soft voice asked.

"It's your man," I answered. I heard her unlocking the door. When Goddess opened it, she damn near jumped in my arms and knocked me over. She wrapped her thick ass legs around my waist and placed kisses all over me like she hasn't seen me in months. And I was loving every bit of it. Needless to say, no words were spoken because we got straight to business and hit the sheets. We spent the next two hours sexing one another in every way imaginable.

I woke to the smell of food. When I looked at the clock, it was a little after 6 p.m. which means we slept for over three hours after our sex session. I used the bathroom before joining Goddess in the kitchen. I walked in and wrapped my arms around her waist and kissed her neck.

"Hey babe. What you in here cooking?"

"I'm making steak, mashed potatoes, sweet corn, and Hawaiian rolls," she answered sweetly.

"Damn, that's just what a nigga need right about now, some good ole comfort food," I told her honestly. Even though being here with Goddess helped ease the pain, I was still feeling fucked up over all this shit. I looked her over and her face seemed to be healing pretty well. I couldn't help but worry about her as well.

"Babe, I'm so glad that you're here right now. I was really struggling over the last few days. Like, I killed the man that I was not too long ago in a relationship with. And I just can't shake it. Then, to make matters worse, that was my secretary that was killed in that basement. All of this is overbearing," she cried. Goddess was right; she did kill someone and I knew this wasn't the time to ask, but I needed to know.

"Babe, where the fuck did you learn how to shoot like that?" Goddess just looked at me before laughing.

"Nigga, I'm in here crying my heart out and you worried about where I learned how to shoot? My daddy taught me and Journey when we were little girls. I couldn't have been no more than nine so she had to be eight. He used to take us to the country to shoot. Then, when we were teenagers, he started taking us to the gun range. By then, we were damn near perfect shooters. For our eighteenth birthday, he brought us our own gun. I never thought I would have to use one but boy was I wrong," she stated while stirring the corn.

"Damn, y'all was younger than we were when y'all learned. I guess your dad is really a street legend. Hopefully, that will be the last person you have to kill. But it does make me feel better to know that you know how to protect yourself if you have to. Having a woman that knows how to bust her guns is kinda sexy," I told her licking my lips.

"Make sure you feel the same way if I have to use my gun on you."

"Damn killer, chill with all that. Why would you have to shoot me?" I asked with my hands in the air.

"Boy, sit your dumb ass down and eat this food. You're such a damn clown."

We sat at the kitchen table and talked while eating, I confided in her about what went down over the last few days. For some reason, talking to Goddess was easy and comfortable. She listened well without interrupting me then gave her input without being judgmental. I never opened up to a woman before, but I must admit, it felt kinda nice. Goddess told me that she thought I should try to build a relationship with Tommy in the near future and try to locate his sister for him. I wasn't sure if I was ready for all of that, but I would give it some thought in the near future. After talking for another hour or so, I cleaned the kitchen while she put on a movie for us to watch. We cuddled on the couch and watched movies for the remaining of the night until we both fell asleep.

CHAPTER 8

Goddess

Three months later

It's been exactly three months since I was kidnapped and almost raped by my ex, but with the help for Princeton, I was coming along pretty good. My dad and I were back to normal and it took me a while to understand where he was coming from. We were now back to our daddy and daughter dinner dates every Thursday night. My office was finally looking like I wanted it to look. I've been working as a therapist for a month now and I really liked it a lot. I decided to still work at the school twice a week. I just couldn't see myself leaving my families. Since I've been opened, I pretty much had the same four patients but today, I had a new one coming in later this afternoon. My birthday was next Friday and I couldn't wait to celebrate with my family and friends. Turning twenty-five is major for where I'm from. Not only was I turning twenty-five, but I also had my own business. My secretary called my phone and told me someone was here to see me. I wasn't expecting any more patients until the afternoon, but I told her to send them back. I heard a knock on the door and yelled for them to come in. When I looked up, it was Princeton.

"Hello ma'am. I was told you were the woman I need to see to help me through my problems?"

"That's correct? So, what brings you in this morning?" I asked.

"This hard ass dick of mine. See, ever since my beautiful Goddess climbed out of bed this morning, my dick won't seem to deflate and I was wondering if you could help me with my problem?" he asked while picking me up and placing me on my desk. Princeton didn't give me a chance to answer; instead, he hiked up my dress and slid my panties off. He quickly dove into my honey pot and ate sloppily. I knew then he wasn't here to make love, he was here to fuck. After getting me nice and wet, Princeton wasted no time dropping his pants and inserting his thickness inside of me. It didn't take me long to start rocking my hips to meet his every stroke. I wrapped my arms around his and moaned softly into his ear.

"Fuck, you feel so good, baby," I cooed.

"Shit, if y'all gonna fuck at work, at least lock the door," I heard my father say before the door closed. I felt so embarrassed and tried to get off the desk but Princeton wasn't having it.

"Where you going? This my pussy and we ain't stopping until we both cum," he said as he continued to stroke in and out of me. This man was crazy if he thought I was still in the mood for sex after my father just caught me getting my back banged out on the desk. I wanted to stop so bad but the more he stroked in and out of me the more I was starting to forget what just happened.

"Oh God, baby, I'm about to cum," I moaned. Princeton strokes became faster, deeper, and harder. He lifted one of my legs higher and went deeper causing me to cum again. "Shit baby, I'm cumming again!" I yelled a little louder.

"Fuck Goddess, me too," he groaned while emptying his load into me. I was mad because I wanted to stop but my body wanted to keep going. Now, I really felt embarrassed.

"Princeton, how the hell am I supposed to face my daddy after he caught us fucking?"

"Girl, you'll be fine. Your father is a grown man so he knows what grown people do. Besides, he didn't catch you fucking: he caught you getting fucked. That's a big difference. I was all in them guts. Maybe next time, he'll knock or your secretary would do her job and call like she did when I got here." I hated to admit it but he was right. I was still a little embarrassed but I am grown. I called my receptionist and told her should send him back. My dad walked in with a dumb smirk on his face. I could tell he was about to start with his shenanigans.

"Y'all really need to start locking doors around here because that just fucked my mental up. I'm ready to sit in the chair and talk to somebody about what I just saw getting done to my daughter. And Goddess, just a little word of advice, never let anyone come to your workplace and fuck you like that. You should have been fucking *him* like that. He just punked you in your own shit. I thought I taught you better than that." Princeton burst out laughing and I was sick of both of them.

"Dad, you and Princeton about to get put out my office with this foolishness. I'm sorry that you had to see that I really am. Next time, I'll make sure to lock the door."

"Baby girl, I'm just fucking with you. You're a grown-ass woman with your own business. That's what I get for not knocking. Although, your secretary should have told me someone was back here but she was so busy eye-fucking me that she probably forgot." All I could do was laugh because my daddy really didn't have any filter, none whatsoever. Princeton kissed my lips before leaving.

"Dad, what brings you here anyway?"

"Actually, I was in the area looking for a building to open up a Café plus, I wanted to know if you had plans tonight?"

"I didn't know you wanted to open a Café. And how did the search go? And no, I don't have plans tonight. Wassup?"

"I need for you and your sister to stop pass the house tonight around 7 pm. I need to talk to y'all about something. And as far as the café, I think I found a building about six doors down from here. I checked it out and I actually like it. I'm just waiting to have it inspected to make sure everything is up to code before I sign on the dotted line."

"Cool sounds nice and yes, I'll be there. Is everything okay?"

"Yup. Just wanna talk to my girls. Let me get out of here. The inspection guy should be there in a few minutes. I love you, baby girl."

"I love you, too, daddy."

The morning flew by and it was now time to take my lunch break. I didn't feel like going out so I ordered some Chinese and ate in my office while checking emails. My heart started beating faster when I read an email from Camden High school inviting me to Samantha's birthday memorial celebration tomorrow. Her death seemed to hunt me all the time and I always worried someone was gonna come ask me questions about me being there when she was killed. I found out on the news that the house I was in was hers. The news declared her death as a break-in gone wrong. Wasn't quite sure where they got that shit from. I decided not to reply just yet. It was bad enough I felt some type of way whenever I went to the job and she wasn't there, so I knew I couldn't go and celebrate her birthday. My lunch break was over so I cleaned my desk off and used the bathroom before my next client.

When my client walked in, she had a familiar way about her, but I couldn't put my finger on it. She sat across from me and stared at me. A single tear escaped down her face.

"Ma'am, are you okay?" I asked. I said a silent prayer that I wasn't dealing with a nut case.

"Yes, I'm fine, thank you. You're just so beautiful," she said wiping her face.

"So, how may I help you today?" I asked, moving along with my session.

"I don't even know where to begin, but I guess I'll start with my biggest regret that I've been carrying around for damn near 20 years. I don't think I'll ever be able to forgive myself for what I've done," she cried.

"Calm down, Ms. Jones. Would you like to share with me what that regret you're carrying is?"

"I abandoned three people that I loved the most for some fast money. I was young and dumb and always told myself that I was gonna go back for them and before I knew it, twenty years had passed. And I hate myself for what I done and I'm sure they hate me, too." My heart began to race because this story was touching a soft spot and this woman had me all in my feelings listening to her. I stared at the woman and she was simply beautiful with a stained face from her tears. I reached over and grabbed some tissues to hand over to her. She wiped her face and blew her nose.

"Have you ever tried to reach out to either of them? If you don't mind me asking, what's your relationship to the three people you abandoned?"

"I'm so sorry, Goddess. I never meant to abandon you and your sister. I love you girls so much. And I left your father to raise y'all by himself," she cried like a baby. My heart had stopped but I felt the tears running down my face. I had to be tripping because I know she wasn't saying what I thought she was saying. This just couldn't be. There was no way.

"Lady, you're bugging and why the hell is apologizing to me?"

"Goddess, I know this is a lot to take in but it's me. I'm your mother," she cried.

"No. No you don't get to do this to me. Why the fuck is you here at my job? Telling me this shit?" I cried angrily.

"I know that you're angry with me Goddess and I don't blame you. I just couldn't let another day go by without being in your life."

"Are you serious right now? I don't want to be in your life! You left me when I was just a little girl for a man and now you want to come back a week before I turn twenty-five? You have some fucking nerve!" I yelled.

"Goddess, is everything okay?" my dad asked as he walked into my office but stopped in mid-sentence when he locked eyes with the woman claiming to be my mother.

"Andrea?" he asked shockingly. "What the hell are you doing here?" The room fell silent. I grabbed my phone and texted to tell Journey to get to my office ASAP.

"Oh my God, Shaad," she whispered coving her mouth.

"Why the fuck are you here, Andrea? I thought your ass was dead?" my dad stated. The room was very tensed and no one was saying anything to each other. My dad was just staring blankly at the woman claiming to be my mom while silent tears rolled down my face. Twenty minutes later, Journey walked in.

"What's with all the screaming in here?"

"This is what the screaming is about. This woman right here!" My dad yelled pointing at Andrea.

"Oh my God, Journey! You are so beautiful."

"Who the hell is this?" Journey asked.

"This is the woman that gave birth to you and your sister. I wouldn't dare call her your mother because mothers don't abandon their children for a man with money!" my dad snapped.

"I'm sorry y'all but at least let me explain why I left. I know it might not be what y'all wanna hear but it's the truth. I did leave y'all and at first, it was my choice. I had someone willing to take care of me and give me the lavish things that I wanted in life and you just couldn't provide that for me. Shortly after I left, I tried to come back to all three of y'all when I found out that I was pregnant with our son and almost lost my life by the man that I thought loved me. He beat the shit out of me every time I would mention y'all names. He told me that the only kid he was raising was the one I was carrying at the time. And he only said that because he thought it was his baby so I let him believe that. He told me if I came back for y'all he would beat y'all like he beat me. And I just wouldn't have been able to live with that, so I stayed away. Five years later, I called myself running away while he was out of town but was in a terrible accident with our son. I was in a coma and our son was in intensive care for damn near a month."

Journey and I were both crying our eyes out and I could have sworn I saw tears in my daddy's eyes. I wasn't sure if she was telling the truth or not, but I was starting to feel sorry for her. I wasn't sure what to say or how to feel. My entire life I wondered why my mom choose a man over her own children. I wondered what she looked like and if I would ever meet her. Now, all of those questions and wonders I had about her were sitting here in my face and I didn't know what the hell to feel. I was angry with her but listening to her story was causing me to soften up just a little. Then I wondered how the hell my father knew something was wrong and to come here but that was the least of my worries right now.

"Andrea, I can't even look at you right now. You really want me to believe that this is the first chance you had to come back for your girls in twenty fucking years? And are you trying to fucking tell me that I have a fucking son? Is that what you're saying? Answer me got dammit!"

"Rashaad, I'm sorry! I don't know what else to say. But I need you to know that there's not a day that went by that I didn't think about y'all. To this day, you're still the love of my life, Rashaad. When I got out the coma, I begged the doctors to help my fake our death. I just couldn't take it anymore. I knew if I went back, he would have killed me the next time. The doctors felt sorry for me and long story short, the hospital pronounced me dead. He told them to cremate us and just give him the ashes. Two years later, I married the doctor that took care of me and he moved me to Texas and that's where I've been. I still didn't feel like I could come back because I was on the run. I felt like I owed it to my husband to stay since he was the one that saved our lives. Then apparently, two years after my supposedly death, Frank was killed. And then my husband died last year in a car accident. So, there you have it, that's my story"

"Andrea, this is bullshit. You don't get to do this. Stay the fuck away from us. I swear to God, Andrea, you have a lot of fucking nerve pulling this shit on us after all of these years. Let me take a guess, your money hungry ass broke? You need some money? Is that why you're here?" my daddy shouted. He was angry beyond words; I actually think hurt was a better word to use.

"Rashaad, please. I already feel bad as hell and no, I don't need your money. My husband left me pretty well off," she answered.

"We have a brother?" I finally spoke.

"Yes. He's 21 years old. And his name is Ta'shaad."

"Fuck you, Andrea! Get out of here now! You really named your son the name we agreed to name our son? Get the fuck out, Andrea!" he yelled again. If I didn't know any better, I would have thought that my dad was still in love with my mom the way he was acting and looking at her.

"Please, don't do this! I just wanna know my daughters and let them get to know their brother. That's all. Rashaad, contrary to what you believe, he's your son. Just take a DNA and you'll see I'm not lying. I didn't come here to start anything or ask for any handouts. I just want y'all to know him and I want to know my girls and that's it," she cried.

"Just leave your number and if we want to build a relationship with you and him then we will contact you. But please don't come back here again," I stated calmly. She handed me a card but when she went to hand Journey her number, she declined.

"Nah, I'm a little too old for a momma. You should have thought about being my mom when I needed you. I think you're full of shit if you ask me. And if I count correctly, you had about fifteen years free of him but instead, you ran off with another man. Now that both of your men are dead, you're back hoping to get your daughters back and rekindle with my dad? Yeah, I'm on to you but that shit isn't gonna happen so fuck you and your son Andrea because we, neither of us, needs you," Journey spat before walking out. I wasn't surprised that Journey felt that way. Hell, I felt the same way but I wasn't gonna say that shit out loud. I just felt like she was still our mom. Well, she was the woman who gave us life and to me, that meant something. Andrea stood there with her mouth hanging open.

"Take all the time you need Goddess but if you don't want to get to know me or want me in your life, then I'll understand and I'll just have to live with my mistakes. Again, I'm sorry," she said before walking out of my office.

My dad sat down in front of my desk and wiped his tears from his face. This was the first time I ever saw my daddy crying and it really had me in my feelings. I wished I could help him, but I was confused and hurt my damn self.

I swear if it wasn't one thing it was another. I took Andrea's number and stored it in my phone in case I lost the card. I wasn't sure what to say to my daddy so I said nothing and neither did he. He just sat there starring into space. He finally got up from the chair and looked at me. "I gotta go," was all said before leaving.

Rashaad

When I got a text from Goddess's secretary telling that she thinks that I should come to the office if I was still in the area, it had me flying back downtown. I had just left from the building that I just purchased a few doors down from her office. When I got there, I heard screaming but couldn't really hear what was being said. What I did know was doctor and patient shouldn't have been yelling at one another. When I walked into Goddess's office, I could have sworn I was looking at a ghost when I locked eyes with Andrea. I had a million different emotions flowing through my body but the only emotion that showed was my anger. Andrea was still as beautiful as the day I first met her. And even though I was pissed and caught off guard, I would be lying if I said a part of me wasn't glad to see her. And hearing her tell us why she left had me wanting to kill an already dead nigga, but I couldn't let that show. Andrea still didn't get a pass because like Journey said, what happened to the other fifteen years? Seeing my girls crying over her really had me fucked up in the head. When I heard that she got married and supposedly had my son that she raised with another man crushed my heart. After Andrea left, I never took another woman serious and she got married. Andrea was the only woman I saw myself marrying. I just recently thought about giving the love thing a second shot. Then, here she comes popping up out of thin air. I just don't trust it and I didn't trust her ass.

I knew I needed to make sure my girls were okay. I also knew that I shouldn't hinder their decision to get to know Andrea if that's what they wanted to do. I know my girls and they are gonna want to know her once they get over the shock and initial hurt. They grew up without a mother then she pops up so they gonna wanna give a shot. But I need to talk to Andrea first to make some shit clear to her. I was having dinner prepared for my girls tonight and now I wasn't sure if I should even still have them over. But then again, I can't let Andrea come back and change our lives in a day. I shot both of them a text letting them know I still wanted them to come over. Andrea really had my head fucked up big time I could hardly think straight.

Later that night

The girls arrived at exactly 7 p.m. When they walked in, I hugged both of them tightly probably more tightly than I have in a long while.

"How's my girls?" I asked trying to lighten the mood.

"We're okay, daddy, but I am curious about what tonight is about?"

"You'll find out in due time. Would y'all like something to drink?"

"After today's events, hell yeah I want something to drink! Just bring out a whole bottle of wine," Goddess blurted. We sat at the table and I brought the wine like she asked.

"Well girls, the reason why I brought you here tonight is because I want you to meet someone special. Her name his Shantae. She was my bartender at the club in Atlanta. We used to hook up whenever I went there but the last few visits they made me realize that I had more feelings then I thought I did. After talking, we decided to give it a shot, so we've been seeing one another for about three months now. I moved her up here so we didn't have to travel to see one another and now I want my favorite ladies to meet her. She should be here any moment."

"Wow daddy. It's about damn time that you got your groove back. Because you were too old to be a player. I'm happy and I'm good with her as long as she makes you happy. And I guess it's safe to say this one knows how to suck dick?" Journey said causing me and Goddess to laugh.

"Yeah dad. I'm happy for you, too. I wish you well. I can't wait to meet her. But do you think it's a good idea moving forward with her since mom is back around?" Goddess asked, catching me off guard.

"Why the hell would that matter to him?" Journey asked.

"Because, it's obvious that dad is still in love with mom. I can see it in his face. Why else did you think he never settled down with another woman? And what I find crazy is after twenty years, he's finally ready to move on and the love of his life pops back up. It could be a sign, I'm just saying," she stated while sipping her wine.

"Wow, that makes sense, daddy. Is that true? Are you still in love with your baby momma?" Journey asked laughing. I wondered what the hell got into these girls. They were acting drunk, but I only saw them drink one glass of wine.

"To answer y'all question, I'll always love Andrea, but I couldn't be with her at this point so yes, I'm going to move forward with Shantae and yes, she knows how to suck dick, lick balls, and eat ass, too, so she's the one."

"Eww daddy! You get your ass ate?" Goddess blurted.

"Hell yeah, I get my ass ate! That shit feels good as hell," I told them while laughing. The buzzer went off and I knew that it was Shantae. I walked over to let her in. "Y'all asses better behave y'all selves," I warned.

"Hey baby," Shantae greeted me with a kiss on the lips.

"Hey baby," I greeted back. "These are my two heartbeats. This is Goddess and this here is Journey. Girls, this is my lady, Shantae," I introduced.

"Hi, it's finally nice to meet you lovely ladies. You're all he talks about and now I can see why. Y'all are beautiful beyond words."

"Thank you and it's finally nice to meet you as well. My daddy has spoken very highly of you. My dad seems to be happy with you so welcome to the family," Goddess spoke.

"Thanks, baby. I really appreciate that. Your father is a very special man and makes me extremely happy," Shantae replied. For the remainder of the night, we all sat, talked, and laughed. For some reason, all I could think about was Andrea. I also kept replaying what Goddess said earlier about Andrea being the love of my life. This shit was fucking with me in the worst way imaginable. After the girls left, I sat and talked with Shantae, but I guess she could tell that something was heavy on my mind.

"Baby, what's wrong? You seem a little off tonight," Shantae asked. I wasn't sure if I was ready to open up to her, but I also didn't feel the need to keep any secrets so I felt like I needed to keep it one hundred with her.

"Listen, you're right. Something is wrong with me. You remember how we talked and I expressed to you how my daughter's mother up and left when they were little girls? Well, out of the blue today, she popped up at Goddess's job. And it has all of us on edge. I have so many different emotions running through me at once. I haven't seen or heard from her since the day she walked out on us so I'm a little fucked up in the head right now. I honestly thought she was dead," I expressed.

"Wow, that's crazy. I can see why y'all would be on edge and emotional. If you don't mind me asking, what did she have to say for herself?"

"Nah, you good, baby. You can ask whatever you want to ask. Long story short, she said she was abused the entire time and couldn't come back for the girls because he threatened that if she came and got them that he would beat them, too. She claimed the only way she could get out of it was to fake her death. But that was five years after she left so for the other ten years, she was living a happily married life and even had a son that she claims to be mine. And now that the guy she that left us for and her ex-husband are both dead, suddenly she's back. I just don't trust it. My girls are grown-ass successful women and doesn't need this right now and neither do I," I expressed honestly.

"Wow, this is a lot to take in and I can honestly say I don't know what to say."

"I know, baby. I'm just all over the place with this. I don't want her to come and add more hurt to their lives. They had to deal with never having a mother or a stepmother. Then boom, you just pop up out the blue and expect what?"

"Yeah, this shit is crazy. Rashaad, do you still love her?"

"Honestly, I always have. I planned to spend my life with her then she left me for a nigga that had more money than me. That just left me having to make a life for me and the girls so I started selling drugs. I was just lucky enough to be good at what I did and was able to make enough money to get out the game sooner than most niggas could. And I was able to go legit."

"Look Rashaad, I love you, I do and I would love to be with you. But I really think you need to seek out your feelings for your daughters' mom. I know this will take time but I'm willing to wait for you to figure out if there's anything there for you and your daughters' mother. If it's not, then I'll be here as your girl and future wife. But if not and you choose to be with her, then please know that this has been the best three months as your girlfriend that I've ever had with any man. I've waited all this time, I can wait longer. I love you Rashaad and don't try to fight me on this. All I want you to do is take me to your bedroom and make love to me until the sun comes up. I need this to hold me over until you figure out what you have going on. You're a man that deserves to be happy even if it's not with me," Shantae told me kissing me on the lips. Nothing else was said between the two of us. I picked her up and carried her to my room and did everything that you could do sexually to someone's body.

The next morning when I woke up, Shantae was gone. I set up my bed and replayed the last twenty-four hours of my day in my head over and over again. I knew deep down that I would probably never be able to be with Andrea, but I did know it was time to close that chapter in my life once and for all and that would require a clear mind and heart. The fact that Shantae was willing to wait for me while I explore with another woman let me know that she was all the woman I needed in due time. I headed to the bathroom to handle my hygiene. I had a meeting at my new building in two hours. I sent both my girls a text to check up on them and they both replied that was pretty good. I knew they would need time to process all of this. If I didn't know anything else, I knew I had to find out if the boy was really my son.

After I got dressed, I headed Downtown. I planned to stop pass Goddess's office if she wasn't busy. When I got in the area, I called and she told me I could stop by for a moment. I walked in her office that was filled with a bunch of flowers.

"Where the hell did all of these come from?"

"Princeton sent them. He's trying to cheer me up. He even sent an edible fruit basket. He was really worried about me when I told him about mom."

"Honestly, I'm worried about you and your sister which is one of the reasons I'm here. I'm not sure if you plan to get to know your mom or not, but I wouldn't be mad if you wanted to. She is your mother. My only request is that you let me talk to her first. So give me her number and after my meeting next door, I'll call and see when she and I can meet. I just don't want y'all to get hurt," I told her.

"Dad, I understand. Here's her number but dad, please be careful," Goddess stated handing me the card that Andrea gave her. "Dad, did the building pass inspection?"

"Yup. I brought it. I'm meeting the contractors down there in a few to go over the minor things I want done in there."

"Dad, I just want you to know that I'm extremely proud of you. I love you, daddy."

"Thanks, Princess. I love you more than words could ever express. I'll see you later." After I left the meeting, I sat in my car and made the phone call I never imagined making. The phone rang until the machine came on and just as I was about to leave a message, my line beeped and it was her calling back.

"Hello? Did someone call Andrea?" her sweet voice answered. My words got caught in my throat and I couldn't speak. "Hello?"

"Hey Andrea, its Rashaad. Do you have a minute?" I asked

"Hi Rashaad! Yes, I have a minute. I'm glad you called."

"I would like to meet up to talk to you whenever you have a chance," I told her.

"Are you free now?" she asked.

"Actually, I am. I was about to go get something to eat from Olive Garden in Cherry Hill if you would like to join me."

"That's sounds like a plan. I'll meet you there in about fifteen minutes."

"Aight cool." I disconnected the call and headed to Olive Garden. I got to my destination in 10 minutes. For some reason, I was getting nervous. When I walked in, Andrea was already sitting down. I walked over to the table and she had already ordered drinks.

"I hope you don't mind but I ordered your drink if this is still your favorite."

"Thanks and yeah, it's still my favorite and only drink," I told her. "But I won't pretend that I trust you so I'll drink it after you drink," I told her seriously. Andrea just stared at me with a blank expression before picking up the glass and drinking some then slid it back to me.

"So, wassup? I'm a little surprised to hear from you after yesterday."

"Well, what the hell did you expect from me when you came barging back into our lives twenty damn years later? Were you expecting a welcome home party? But let me get to the point. I can't stop the girls from getting to know or building a relationship with you if they so choose to. But I will tell you this; if you here for games or further hurt them, then walk away because I will kill you myself if you cause more hurt to them then you've already have. So, I hope you not here on no bullshit because I'm not the same nigga you was with twenty years ago. I'm a street legend and I'm a big deal. So I have enough money and power to wipe you from this earth leaving nothing left of you except ashes. Those girls are my every fucking thing, Andrea. I raised them alone with a little assistance from my sister when I needed it. So if you here on bullshit, walk away now and never look back and I mean it," I warned.

"Hi, are you ready to order?" the waitress asked. We both placed our orders then got back to our conversation.

"Look Rashaad. I know that this is difficult, but I swear, I'm not on no bullshit. You have my word. But what do you mean you're a street legend? I know you're not a drug dealer?" she asked.

"It means exactly what the fuck I said and the last time I recalled, you like drug dealers right? That's who the fuck you left your family for right?" I asked angrily.

"Rasheed, please calm down. I know that you're angry and hurt, but I'm not gonna keep letting you disrespect me like I'm a nobody." I thought about what Andrea said and she was somewhat right. I needed to just chill and hear her out and give her a chance.

"Look, you're right. This is just new to me and it's a little too much. You hurt my fucking soul when you left, Andrea. I had to take care of the girls by myself. I became the biggest fucking drug dealer there was to care for them and I did a damn good job. I raised them to the best of my ability. I put both of them through school and they have multiple degrees, so I think I did a pretty good job."

"I'm so sorry Rashaad and I can't thank you enough for raising them to be the women that they are today. I feel like shit that I wasn't a part of their success. But I would love to be there for future things."

"They won't make a move without my go ahead, so I'll let them know that it's okay. Journey isn't gonna be as easy to crack as Goddess will be. She's a lot like you while Journey is more like me. She's stubborn and doesn't trust easily and although they both have mouth, Journey will crush your soul with her words just like me. I'm just giving you a heads up."

"Thanks, Rashaad. I really appreciate what you're doing. So, what about you? How hard will it be to get you to trust me?" It was something about the way she asked that sent chills down my body.

"This is about you and the girls not me. Now, when can I meet him so I can get this test over with?" I asked changing the subject. Andrea just smiled before answering.

"You can meet him today if you would like. He's at home. You can follow me to my house which is only five minutes from here," she stated.

After I paid for the bill, we both headed out the door. I was impressed. Andrea definitely looked like she was doing well for herself just by the Jaguar she was driving. We pulled up in front of a beautiful home and I was even more impressed. I guess she wasn't here for money. As we walked towards her door, my stomach was doing backflips. I wasn't sure what to expect from meeting him but the thought of having a son kinda had me excited. I've always wanted a son. But I refused to have kids with another woman.

"Ta'shaad, I'm home and someone's here to see you." When he walked down the steps, I almost lost my breath. He looked exactly like me and there was no way in hell ole boy thought this was his kid.

"Wow," was all I could say at the moment.

"So, you're my dad, huh? I can't believe that I'm finally meeting the man that I've heard so much about. Well, it's nice to finally meet you."

"Well, I hope you've only heard good things about me and it's a pleasure to meet you as well," I told Ta'Shaad while shaking his hand. "Look, I'm a straight shooter and I'm sure if your mother has told you about me that she had to tell you the situation I had no idea that you existed and before I get too attached I would like for us to get a DNA just so I can confirm you're really my son and then we'll go from there," I told him I honestly.

"Yeah, she told me all about it and I'm good with you getting a DNA cuz I completely understand. I'm ready whenever you are, dad. And to answer your other question, yes, she has only spoken good things about you. As a matter of fact, she spoke so highly of you; I was starting to think she was dating Jesus." I couldn't help but to laugh at his remark.

After sitting and talking to him for a few hours, I learned that he was a clothing designer looking to open up his own store. We had a lot more in common than I expected. We planned to get the test done by the end of the week so we can get it over with. I took his number and gave him mine and then headed out the door. This shit was becoming overwhelming. The last twenty years of my life, I thought I only had two daughters and their mother was dead but come to find out, she's very much alive and telling me that I have a son. As soon as I left, I headed straight home to pour myself a double shot of Henny and I smoke a blunt. Deep down, I know I have to keep my distance away from Andrea because just that quick, things were starting to feel the way they used to when we were together. And that shit just couldn't happen.

One-week later Friday morning

Today was the day we were going to take the DNA test. I couldn't lie and say I wasn't nervous as hell, but I was anxious. I wasn't sure If I was anxious to get it over with so I could prove that Andrea was a liar. Or if I was anxious because I was happy about the fact that I may have a son. We met up at the diagnostic center to take the test and I paid extra to have it rushed. They told me I should have the results within 2 days if not sooner. I told the girls I was getting the test done. I didn't want them to get attached to him until we knew what was what. After we left on the diagnostic place, we went our separate ways. I had so much shit to do. I had to make sure everything was set in stone for Goddess' party tomorrow night. Journey and Latrice were handling the cake while I handled everything else. Princeton offer to help but I told him I wanted to do this party for my daughter on my own. The only thing I needed him to do was get Goddess there, since it was a surprise party. She thought we were going out to a fancy dinner. I couldn't believe my firstborn was turning twenty-five in less than 24 hours. It seemed like it was just yesterday that she was born. After I was finished running all my errands and making sure everything was straight for tomorrow, I decided to go pay Shantae a visit. I was missing her ass like crazy. I knocked on the door and when she answered, she looked surprised to see me.

"Oh my God ,Rashaad, what are you doing here? I wasn't expecting to see you anytime soon," she stated.

"Well, I'm here. I was missing you like crazy girl plus, I came to give you an update on everything that's been going on."

"I miss you, too, Rashaad. So, how's everything?"

"Well, for starters, I finally sat and talked with Andrea. Well, more like threatened her. I needed to make sure that she wasn't here on no bullshit. I told her she was here on some funny shit she might as well leave now because if she hurt my daughters, I would kill her myself. So far, she seems pretty genuine about really just wanted to get to know them and having a relationship with her girls. My supposed-to-be son, he looks just like me but that doesn't mean anything so we went and took a test today the results should be back sometime this week."

"Damn babe, this is a lot. So, what are you going to do if he's yours?"

"It's not really much I can do but try to build a relationship from here on out. The years I've lost I can't get back. I have no idea what type of upbringing that he had so all we can do is move forward. All of this is just a lot to take in. Twenty damn years has just been me and my two girls so that's all I know. I don't know how to share them with their mother or brother. Well, I'm having a hard enough time trying to share them with their men," I told her honestly.

"Rashaad, I understand everything that you're saying. All you can do is take it one day at a time, but I'm sure everything will work itself out and the things that you don't know you're going to have to learn. I just hope that she's here for the right reasons. I would hate to see the three of you get hurt and I would hate to see you behind bars for killing her ass," Shantae said while laughing.

"This is why I love you so much," I told her by placing a kiss on her lips. "I know things may be a little awkward right now but you know you're still more than welcome to come to the birthday party with me tomorrow. I would actually love to have you on my arm. I haven't decided if I should invite Andrea, yet, but even if I do, I would like for you to be there. If it's too much or uncomfortable for you, I understand completely."

"If you don't mind me expressing my opinion, I think that you should extend the invitation to Andrea and if you want me on your arms baby, then I'll be on your arm. What time should I be ready?"

"I'll pick you up around 7:15 pm. The party starts at 8 pm."

"Okay baby. I'll see you tomorrow." I left Shantae's house feeling like a lucky man. After running a few more errands, I took my ass in the house and did a little work from home before calling it a night.

CHAPTER 9

Goddess

I awoke this morning getting some birthday head followed by dick. Once we were finished, we both took a shower and got dressed. Princeton as taking me to breakfast before I linked up with Journey and Latrice to get pampered all day. We pulled up to Perkins in Morristown for some bomb ass breakfast food. This was one of my favorite breakfast spots. After ordering our food, we just sat and talked. I wondered where the hell we were eating at for dinner that I had to dress up. Not that I cared because all I wanted was to be with my family. After breakfast, Princeton dropped me off at Journey's house. I didn't even bother to knock. I used my key to get in.

"Journey, where you at?"

'Damn bitch, I'm right here. Happy birthday, Goddess," she said hugging me tightly.

"Thanks, bitch. You ready to go?'

"Yup. Latrice just texted and said she's outside. Where we going first, to the nail salon?"

"You already know it."

When we got in the car, Latrice played Birthday Bitch and we cut the fuck up in the car. When we made to the nail salon, my nail tech Keith, immediately started getting my water ready for my feet. The three of us sat next to one another getting our feet done and running our mouths.

"What's the name of the restaurant we going to?" I asked.

"Bitch, I forgot. You know your daddy bougie. I just know it's in Voorhees," Journey answered.

"Do y'all think he invited y'all, mom?" Latrice asked.

"Who knows, but I hope not. I don't feel like being around her tonight," Journey expressed.

"I honestly wouldn't mind if she was there. She seems okay so far. She texts me every morning. I actually would love to get to know her. I know we're grown but hell, grown people still need their mothers. Hell, we still need daddy. I would be lost with him," I stated honestly.

"Honestly, a part of me would like to get to know her. The other part of me is too hurt to wanna know her. I've texted her a few times but it just seems weird and forced.

"Well, I'm just gonna let it flow. I'm not forcing shit. I know she's beautiful as hell. I could see why daddy was in love with her. Besides, daddy has a great judge of character so if he was with her and allowed her to have two of his kids, then at one point she had to be something special. Up into two weeks ago, he never thought about entertaining another woman and he never had more kids."

"Yeah, I guess you're right. I do know one thing; Ta'Shaad looks just like his ass."

"Yeah, he do. I think daddy knows. He just needs to make sure. At least if he is his son, we'll have a brother," I told Journey. The three of us just sat and talked while we got our Mani, Pedi, and eyebrows done. I loved those bitches with everything in me. They were truly ride or die. Once we were done, we ended up at Applebee's for lunch before our hair appointments. I wasn't quite sure what I was getting done to my hair, but I knew I wanted something different. After eating and fucking around at the restaurant, it was time for our appointment. I was amazed how quick the day was going. If my ass were at work the day would be dragging. I was glad that we didn't have to wait to get started when we got to the salon.

"Hey girl, wassup with you?' my stylist asked.

"Shit, tryna get right for my birthday. My family taking me to some fancy-ass restaurant tonight."

"Happy birthday, girl! Are you getting the usual?' she asked.

"Nope. I think I want something different tonight. I think I want some bundles and shit. Just hook your bitch up," I told her.

"I got you bitch. Just one question: did you still want you side shaved?" I thought about it for a moment before answering.

"You know what? I do."

"That's all I needed to know." Almost three hours later I was just getting finished. When she handed me the mirror, I was in awe with what I saw. She shaved the right side of my hair off and added three lines in the cut and gave me some pretty bouncy, long, curly tracks. The color was like a burnt orange and I loved it. This shit had me looking like a million bucks. I knew Princeton was gonna lose his damn mind when he saw me tonight. I saw Latrice and Journey walking towards me. When they got close, all I heard was Journey's big ass mouth.

"Oh my God, bitch, you look stunning! My sister cuter than your sister," she sang loud as hell in the middle of the salon. People were looking at us like we were crazy, especially, when we started popping our asses to our own music.

"Thanks, bitch! I love y'all hair, too. We cute as fuck point blank period. Maybe after dinner we should hit the club. I'm in the mood to shake my ass tonight," I suggested.

"Shit, you know I'm wit it. We about to be lit," Latrice stated. I looked at my phone and realized it was already 5 pm.

"Shit y'all, we gotta go. Y'all know we take long as hell to get dressed plus, I know I'm gonna have to give this nigga some pussy before we leave tonight," I said causing them to laugh. When they dropped me off, Princeton wasn't home yet. I had been staying at his house with him damn near every night for the last month. It felt nice waking up to him every day.

I walked into the room to lay my clothes out, but when I in, there was a complete outfit laid out all the way down to the shoes. He even had bra and panties laid out for me. I noticed he left me a note on the nightstand.

"Hey baby, I know you're wondering where I am, but I decided to get dressed at Perry's house and just pick you up. I already know you gonna look good as fuck and if we're in the same house, your dad would be mad at me because we would never make dinner because we would be fucking all night long. So I'll see you around 7 p.m. I love you, baby. Ps. I hope you like the outfit. You're gonna look stunning."

All I could do was smile at the note. I took my shower and applied light makeup on before getting dressed. Once I was fully dressed, I was ready to fuck myself because this outfit was everything. I was rocking a lace Bodycon one-piece pants romper that only covered my most precious parts. The front was low cut all the way down to my stomach. It was grown and sexy. My shoes were black opened toed heels with silver diamonds. I walked over to grab some silver jewelry and noticed that I had a brand-new set that matched the shoes. Princeton had really outdone himself. I couldn't wait to get him home alone tonight. I may have to skip the club and come straight home with my man.

After I let my hair down, I applied some lip gloss to my lips and spritzed. I heard the doorbell and wondered who it was being as though Princeton had keys to his own home. I grabbed my clutch and my phone before heading to the door. "Just a minute," I yelled.

When I opened the door, my breath got caught in my throat when I locked eyes with my man. Princeton looked like he just stepped out of a magazine. He wore a custom-made black suit with a silver shirt with black and silver shoes. His hair was cut lower than he normally kept it showing off them perfect deep waves. His full beard was trimmed to perfection. His jewelry sparked and enhanced his looks even more. I literally felt the juices flowing from out of me. Thank God for pantie liners.

"Holy shit Goddess, you look so fucking good right now, you need to bring your ass out this house before you make us miss the entire dinner. I love you hair you are truly a Goddess.

"Thanks babe. You looking dapper your damn self. I think we better get going because I'm already wet and horny," I told him. We both bit our bottom lips at the same time.

"Yeah, it's time to go," Princeton demanded. He grabbed my arm and escorted me to the car. He opened my door and waited for me to get in before closing it. The sexual tension in the car could be felt a mile away and I couldn't wait until we got to the restaurant to put a little distance between us because I felt like I was being tortured right now. This was the first time since I've known about this dinner that I didn't want to go.

We pulled up a secluded area that did looked kinda fancy. I couldn't quite make out the name of the place but it looked elegant. Now, I just had to get through the night with my family so I could get home to my man. Princeton let me out the car and put his arm into mine and we walked towards the restaurant. When we walked up to the door, he opened it and let me walk in first.

"Surprise!" everyone yelled. I just covered my mouth because I was indeed surprised; these negroes really managed to pull off a surprise party.

"Oh my God, I can't believe y'all threw me a party! I'm so happy right now," I expressed. I looked around the room and saw a little bit of everybody there, even people I didn't know. I looked over in the corner and my mom was also there along with my might be brother. I felt a single tear fall from my eye. I was just so overjoyed with happiness right now. Not to mention, everyone looked so nice.

After hugging my dad and sister, I made my way around the room to greet everyone. I walked over to my mom and she looked stunning. I couldn't believe how beautiful she was. I pulled her in for a hug and when she wrapped her arms around me, the tears poured freely from my face and before I knew it, she crying with me. Her embrace was warm and I didn't want to let her go. I finally knew what it feels like to be hugged by your mother and it felt so good. I finally pulled back and she looked at for a few moments.

"Goddess, you are beautiful. I can't believe I missed out on your life. I'm so sorry," she said hugging me again.

"Thanks, you look beautiful as well," I replied. I finally hugged Ta'Shaad before moving around the room. Princeton was now standing by my side and I needed that.

"Come here, baby. I have someone I would like for you to meet." We walked over to a table that seated a woman and a man. I could tell by looking at the woman that she had to be Princeton's mother because he looked like the male version of her. "Goddess, this is my mother Janet and my dad Tommy," he introduced.

"It is a pleasure to finally meet you, Goddess. Now I can see why my son is whipped and in love. You're breathtaking honey."

"Thank you so much and I'm just as whipped and in love with him as he is with me," I stated honestly.

"I like the sound of that. You did good with this one, son," she stated.

"It's a pleasure to meet you as well," his father said.

"You too," I told him.

For the rest of the night, I enjoyed myself and the food was great. The music was even better. I made it my business to mingle with everyone and we were having a ball. This was the best birthday ever and I'll never forget.

"May I have everyone's attention?" my dad voiced over the loudspeaker. "For everyone that knows me knows that my girls are my pride and joy. Goddess, I just wanted to tell you and everyone in this entire room how much you mean to me. From the first day I laid eyes on you twenty-five years ago, I've been in love with you. You were my firstborn and my first true love. I am so proud of the woman that you have become. I know I don't always agree with the decisions that you make but because I raised you, I know that in the end, everything will work out just fine. Keep up the good work. No matter when or how I die, I know that I will have a smile on my face because with daughters like you, I have no reason to frown. I love you, Goddess and if it's not too much, I would love to have this dance with you," he spoke holding his hand out for me to join him. My dad led me to the dance floor as the song "Daddy" by Beyoncé played through the speakers. Of course my emotional ass was crying tears of joy as we danced to the perfect song. I loved my father more than anything in this world, and no one would ever replace the love I have for him. As soon as the song ended, my daddy kissed me on the cheek.

"I love you, Princess."

"I love you, too, daddy." Everyone was clapping and cheering when another familiar voice spoke.

"Can I have everyone's attention once again? I promise I won't be long. Goddess, can you come sit right here for a moment?" Princeton asked. I walked over to the chair that he pulled into the middle of the floor and sat down. I hoped he wouldn't say anything to make me cry because I was sick of crying for one night. But knowing Princeton, he would be the one that would make me laugh. "First, I would like to say Happy birthday."

"Thank you."

"From the first day I met you, you had me doing shit that I would never do in my life. As long as I've been living, I've never jumped in front of a bullet for anyone. I run from them because who wants to be shot right? But that night, I was willing to get shot for a woman I didn't even know and I did get shot and the crazy thing about it is, I'll take a thousand more bullets for you. I said that to say, I was right; there was something special about you and six months later, you still got me doing shit that I never thought I'd do. For example, I never thought that I would be standing in the middle of this floor giving this speech in front of all these people. I also wouldn't have asked a woman to take my last name until now. Goddess Le'Ann Jenkins, will you please do me the honors and allow me to change your last night? Will you be Mrs. Goddess Le'Ann Hughes?" he asked, dropping to the floor on one knee and sliding the most gorgeous diamond on my hand. I covered my face with my hands and tried to stop the waterworks but they fell freely down my face. My words were caught in my throat so I just simply nodded my head until I could get the words out.

"Yes! I'll marry you, Princeton Hughes," I answered placing a kiss on his lips. He deepened the kiss and that led to us making out on the dance floor like it was just the two of us in the room.

"You have about twenty minutes to show off that ring and be congratulated then you need to go down those steps to the left and wait for me. I'm about to tear that pussy up," Princeton whispered in my ear. All I could do was giggle. I knew some people may have felt like it was too soon for us to get married but we would plan our wedding at least a year away if not longer. I wanted something extravagant.

My father was the first one to walk over to congratulate us and threaten Princeton. My daddy was a hot ass mess, but I loved everything about him. After talking to everyone including my mother, I snuck off to do the nasty with my fiancée for damn near a half hour and I honestly didn't care what anyone thought about me getting some dick at my birthday party with my soon-to-be husband. After busting two nuts each, we cleaned ourselves up and rejoined the party. My dad was on the dance floor bumping and grinding with his girlfriend with his nasty ass daughter on the side of him doing damn near the same shit with Perry. I was ready for this party to be over so I could make love to my man all night long. The party was finally over and after saying our goodbyes, we headed home.

Six months later
Andrea

I couldn't wait for my plan to come into play. Although, I did have love for my girls, I hated them more. They took my man from me. From the minute I had those girls, Rashaad paid more attention to them than he did me and I wasn't having it. So, I left his ass to raise his precious little girls. The only thing that threw a monkey wrench into my plans was when I found out that I was pregnant with my son. Everything I told them was damn near a lie. I planned to use my son as a pawn but he was with it. Once Rashaad knew that was his, I knew he would put him in his will once he built a relationship with him. And that's exactly what he did. Now, I just had to get close enough to Rashaad to kill him with this needle. I planned to kill Rashaad and take him from his precious daughters just like they took him from me. It's been exactly three months since Goddess' birthday party and Ta'Shaad has been hanging out with his daddy damn near every day. I've even taken the girls out a few times. The night at the party, I had to watch Rashaad parade around with that bitch he had on his arm all night. And for some reason, that made my blood boil watching him with another woman. My phone rang breaking me from my thoughts.

"Hey baby. I was just about to call you," I answered on the second ring.

"How's everything going? I miss my wife. When are you coming back home? You know that house and car is costing a fortune and our money is gonna run low," my husband said into the phone.

"I know, baby. I miss you, too. I plan to go through with the plan in the next two weeks. Rashaad is having a meeting with his kids tonight to change the paperwork over and add Ta'Shaad into his will so once that's done, I'll call him over or something and give him the needle. Then, we'll be rich and your wife will be back home."

"Okay baby. Andrea, this was the best plan you've ever come up with," my husband praised me.

"Thanks, babe, but you're the doctor. If it wasn't for you providing the drugs, this wouldn't be possible. But let me get off this phone, I love you."

"I love you, too."

CHAPTER 10

Rashaad

"**D**addy, do we have to have a meeting tonight? I have plans with Perry," Journey whined.

"Stop complaining, Journey. That boy must really got some good dick because all you want to do is be stuck up underneath his ass. Those boys got my girls dickmatized, boy I tell you." Journey just rolled her eyes. "Besides, if you must know, everyone is coming." Her face lit up and now she was smiling. "Ever since you been fucking that boy you seem to have a problem doing shit that I ask. Don't start getting sassy with me."

Everyone had finally arrived at the house, but I had everyone come in through my secret garage and catch the elevator up to the house. Once everyone was seated, I pulled out a folder before speaking.

"First, I would like to think everyone for fitting me into their busy schedule tonight so I'm gonna get straight to the point. The reason why I called this meeting is discuss some shit that has been brought to my attention and since we're all family, I thought it would only be right to keep everyone in this room in the loop. It has been brought to my attention that my children's mother is full of shit just as I thought she was," I said pulling my gun out. "Andrea, I told you when we first met up that if you were here on some bullshit and was here to cause more hurt then I would kill you, am I right?"

"Rashaad, what the hell are you talking about? I haven't done anything to you or these girls." I didn't even respond. I just pushed the intercom to the basement. "Bring him up." A couple minutes later, Tommy brought in Andrea's supposedly dead husband. Anger took over my body and I shot that nigga in the head blowing his head right off his shoulders. Everyone was screaming but I didn't care. I told that bitch not to play with me so this was on her. Next, I pointed my gun at my son and as much as it would hurt me to kill one of mine, I couldn't trust him. He was raised by her and she was a snake so fuck him, too.

"Rashaad, please don't do this! Don't kill my son! You would kill your own son?" Andrea pleaded. Before I could respond, bullets ripped through Ta'shaad and I watched him take his last breath. Andrea let out scream that I've never heard before. I looked around the room to see who had pulled the trigger and it was Perry. I was kinda glad but it was gonna kill me to have to kill my own flesh and blood. Andrea got up to run towards me while yelling but then quickly hit the floor and was now lying in her own blood. I looked up and both of my girls had their guns out. I felt bad for them. I knew that they would live with her death for the rest of their lives.

"Daddy, no women and no children. We couldn't let your break your own rules for her but please tell us what the fuck just happened? What did she do?" Goddess cried still holding the gun.

"She came back to kill me. She only wanted me to know about my son so he could be added to my will and my estate. She planned to go back home to her husband that she lied about being dead. The three of them planned it together so they had to die together. I'll explain to y'all more but right now, I gotta get rid of these damn bodies," I told them.

I already had my niggas that handled shit like this for me waiting for me to give them the word. I made the call and gave them the code word. Goddess had her face buried into Princeton's chest crying. I knew this was gonna kill them. I wished I coulda done it without them knowing, but I have never lied to my girls before and I wasn't gonna start now. I was just glad that they had real men. I fucked with Princeton and Perry the long way. Once the cleanup crew came and did their job it was just us left. I told the crew to set it up as a robbery gone wrong. They knew what to do. I passed my girls a folder then played them the recordings and camera footage that I had collected. See, after about a month, some shit just didn't seem right so I started doing some digging and one night, I invited Andrea and my son over to sign some fake documents just long enough to put cameras in. I also had someone bug her car. So, when I heard and saw the shit she was doing, I knew I had to get her before she got us.

Two hours later, everybody left and I just prayed that my girls would be able to get through this sooner than later. I sat there with my own private thoughts. I was hurting bad. I had to kill my son and his momma which was once the love of my life. I'm just glad I didn't have to be the one that pulled the trigger because that shit would have really killed me. I actually liked the little nigga but he was raised by a snake so he had to go, too. I didn't feel like staying in the house tonight so I went and spent the night with Shantae. I needed to feel her touch and comfort.

One month later
Goddess

I decided to walk down to my daddy's café for some wings and fries. My dad opening a café on this block was the best thing he could've done. Business was booming and the food was delicious. Princeton was meeting me there so we could eat and go over some last-minute wedding stuff. When I walked in, I found us a table in the corner and ordered our food and drinks. About twenty minutes later, Princeton joined me.

"Hey baby. Wassup," he said kissing me on the lips.

"Hey, baby. I ordered our food already."

"Good looking out babe cause a nigga is hungry as hell."

Our wedding was three months away and I couldn't wait. I was excited, nervous, and scared at the same. We tried to plan the wedding ourselves but that shit wasn't working so I hired a wedding planner and things seemed to be running smoothly. Our food came in and I was like four wings in when it felt like I had to throw up. I jumped up from the table and ran to the bathroom barely making it to the toilet before vomit flew out of my mouth. Once I was finished, I washed my mouth out and went back to the table.

"Babe, what the hell happened?"

"I don't know. I had to throw up. Maybe I was probably eating too damn fast. Anyway, about this wedding, don't forget the cake tasting is tomorrow," I reminded him.

"I won't and you know I have to go down to Atlantic City tomorrow to meet with these contractors. Yeah babe, I know we should only be an hour. We shouldn't take that long to decide on a cake. Then you can go do what you need to do." After a second try at my wings, I was still feeling like I had to throw up so I gave up. I wasn't sure if it was the extra sauce I ordered or what but those wings just wasn't agreeing with me.

I took my ass back to work because I had a patient coming in about ten minutes after. Princeton walked me back to my job then he got in the car and left. I walked into my office and waited for my patient to come in. This was a new one so these sessions are usually a little longer. When my patient walked in, she looked around the room first before sitting down. She was pregnant and looked like she was about four months or so.

"Good afternoon. What brings you in today, Aisha?"

"Look, I'm just gonna get to the point. As you can see, I'm pregnant and this is Perry's baby. I'm tired of him avoiding me so I thought I'll just come through you. So can you please tell your sister to let him know that he can't avoid me forever? I'm gonna need some things for the baby."

All I could say to myself was it's always some bullshit.

"Listen here, whatever you have going on with Perry is your business. Don't put my sister in this shit and keep her name outta your mouth. Now, get the fuck outta my office and never return unless you want the shit beat outta you. I can't stand ghetto ass girls."

"Bitch, I would do and say as I please. Fuck you, him, and your sister. Let's see if she stays with his when she finds out he cheated on her and gotta baby on the way. Anyway boo-boo, this office cute, tho," Aisha said while laughing on her way out. I wasn't sure if she was telling the truth or not but what I did know was I needed to talk to my sister and let her know what was what just in case it was true. I doubted though; I couldn't see Perry cheating on my sister with some bird bitch like that but then again, my dad did say the average man would stick his dick in anything that had a pussy.

I wasn't quite sure how she was gonna react when I told her. I was gonna tell Princeton about what happened and maybe Perry would tell Journey himself. The workday seemed longer than usual and I wasn't feeling too well. I really just wanted to go home and lay down. Once I clocked out, I headed straight home and surprisingly, Princeton was already there. When I walked in the house, the smell of food hit my nostrils. I found Princeton and Perry in the kitchen. Shit, I wasn't expecting to see him here.

"Hey baby, how was the rest of your workday?"

"Hey babe. It was pretty good. I wasn't expecting you home this early. And what did you cook? It smells good in here."

"I just made some seafood Alfredo and broccoli. I hope you don't mind, your sister and Perry are gonna stay for dinner."

"Yeah, it's cool. I'm gonna go lay down for a little it. I'll get up when my sister gets here," I told him before walking out the kitchen. When I got to my room, I stripped out of my work clothes and put on some tights and shirt and lay on my bed. I grabbed my little throw cover to over my body and was easing into sleep. I heard the door opened and it was Princeton. He sat down on the bed next to me.

"Baby, are you sure you're okay? It's not like you to come in a take a nap right before dinner."

"Yeah, I'm okay. I guess it's been a long week also, I wasn't expecting to see Perry and Journey today because something happened at the office today when you dropped me off. Somebody named Aisha came to my job and said that she was pregnant by Perry and for me to tell my sister to tell Perry that he can't avoid her forever," I told him. Princeton looked at me like he was waiting for the joke to be over.

"Hell nah! That can't be true. What was her name?"

"She said Aisha and I didn't know if it's true or not, but I know she was pregnant. I have to tell Journey what happened whether it's true or not so he better figure something out," I told him.

"I don't think that shit is true, babe. My brother would have told me if he had a seed on the way and he hasn't said anything about stepping out on Journey but I'll talk to him." I didn't really say much after that. I just wanted to close my eyes until it was time to eat. Princeton got up and left out the room and I closed my eyes. I swore it seemed like minutes later. It was time to get up. I dragged myself out of bed and used the bathroom before joining them in the kitchen.

"Hey, why the hell you sleep at this hour?" Journey asked as soon as I walked into the kitchen.

"I was just a little tired. I think I'm coming down with something. Anyway, wassup with you?"

"Shit, just not too long ago got off work. About to eat here then take my ass home. I have some paperwork to do."

Princeton sat our plates in front of us and I couldn't wait to eat. I decided to wait until dinner was over to say something to Journey about the girl Aisha because I didn't want to ruin dinner. Perry seemed to be a little more quiet than usual so I wasn't sure if Princeton had said something to him about what I told him or not. As soon as we were done eating dinner, I got to the point.

"I'm not the one that usually get into anyone's relationship business but after what happened to today, I feel like I need to say something whether it's true or not. Some girl named Aisha came into my office today and said she's carrying your baby Perry and you couldn't avoid her forever. She was ghetto ass fuck. We had a few words because she put my sister in it and I told her to take that shit up with you. I don't know if it has any truth to it or not, but I didn't appreciate her coming to my job with that bullshit." Perry was wearing a displeasing look on his face and his jaw was clenched.

"What the fuck is she talking about, Perry? Did you get another bitch pregnant?" Journey yelled.

"Look Journey, I don't know what the fuck that girl is talking about. I mean, I did fuck her but that was before you and I got together and I strapped up. So if she is pregnant, that baby can't be mine," he stated. Journey was starting to turn red and I knew I had to say something to calm her down.

"Journey, I was just telling because I didn't want to keep anything from you but before you snap, check into getting your facts before you do anything crazy. I know it's a lot to take in but try to stay calm until you find out what's, what."

"Call her right now on speakerphone," Journey demanded, totally disregarding what I said.

"I'm not calling that girl," he snapped.

"I'm not fucking playing with your ass, Perry. Call her right the fuck now and put it on speaker. I will not deal with no cheating ass nigga and I'm damn sure not about to play step-mommy to a bitch baby that you cheated on me with so call her right fucking now!" she barked. Perry pulled his phone from his pocket and dialed a number. On the second ring, the phone picked up.

"I see you must have gotten my message. Perry, you need to stop playing with me. I'm not about to take care of this baby by myself."

"Aisha, you know fucking well that ain't my baby. We only fucked once and I used a condom. You just tryna start shit with me and my girl because I don't want your ass." She laughed hard. Similar to the laugh she did at my office.

"Nigga, you must be high right now or sitting in front of your girl because you know fucking well we fucked more than some damn once and stop acting like you don't remember the time the condom popped. Don't nobody want you, Perry. I just want you to take of your child. We were just fucking a few weeks ago and now you acting new. Just take care of your child and get the fuck off my phone unless that's what you calling for. What kinda man doesn't claim his child because of a chick?" she chuckled before hanging up the phone.

Before anyone could see it coming, Journey had smacked the shit out of Perry. He was caught off guard and his reflexes were about to hit her back but he caught himself.

"Journey, keep your motherfucking hands off me! You gonna believe some fucking hoe over me? Then fuck you and her! I'm the fuck out," he yelled before storming out of the house. Princeton followed behind while I tried to comfort my sister. I wasn't sure what to believe but what I did know was Perry better find a way to prove the girl to be lying because he would lose Journey forever. Journey has left guys for way less; she wasn't forgiving like most women that get cheated on. The truth was, neither of us were.

"Journey, everything is gonna be okay. The truth will come out," I told her.

"Goddess, for some reason, I believe her. It was just something in her voice that told me she wasn't lying. Even if he isn't the father, I believe that it was more than once which still makes him a liar. I love him so much, but I know I would never be able to forgive Perry if it's true. I have to go. I just want to be alone right now," Journey said leaving out the door. I didn't bother to go after her because I knew how my sister was when she got like this.

For some reason, I was crying and it wasn't even my situation. I started to think about my mom and how these are the moments when every girl needed her mom but we didn't have one because she didn't want us. And then, when she did come back, it was to hurt us even more so we had to kill her. Before I knew it, I was crying like someone had died. I heard the door open and knew it had to be Princeton.

"Baby, why the hell are you in here crying so hard?"

"I don't know. I just started thinking about Journey and my mom and how we killed her. It's just too much," I cried.

"Baby, stop crying. Everything is gonna be okay. You've really been emotional lately. You need to chill baby," Princeton said rubbing my hair. "I think you need to shower and lay down. You apparently didn't have a good day." I couldn't agree more. I got in the shower and didn't even bother to put any clothes on. I just got in the bed. Just before I dozed off, I heard Princeton tell me he would be right back. He had to make a run and just like that, I was knocked out.

Princeton

I had so much going at once that it wasn't even funny. Within the last few months, so much has changed. Me and Perry decided to get out the game because we couldn't find a valid reason to stay in it. We both had enough money to last us a lifetime plus, I wanted to do something legit. I just brought a hotel and casino down in Atlantic City, New Jersey. I'm having it completely remodeled. It's supposed to be completely finished in about six months. My pops and I have been kicking it lately but Perry wasn't too happy about it at first but he finally came around. I knew everyone thought I was crazy for being cool with him being as though he's the one who had my father killed. The truth was, he had valid reasons and there's rules to the game and if you break the rules, you had to be dealt with accordingly; no matter who you were. I wasn't happy about it either, but I had to respect it. Perry and I decided to let Tommy take over the streets and he seemed to be pretty good at running shit so far. I was glad I didn't put a bullet in his head that night. After Goddess and I came from lunch, I decided to cook dinner and invite Perry and Journey over but that was a big mistake. I wasn't sure what was gonna happen between Perry and Journey because when him and I were outside, he admitted to fucking up and that it was possible the baby could be his but he didn't want to lose Journey. He asked me to just keep it between us until he figured shit out. I just hoped that shit didn't come in between me and Goddess.

Something was a little off with Goddess lately. She's been emotional and tired and then at lunch, she ran off to the bathroom. I wasn't sure if it was just stress or if she was just reliving the death of her mother. If I don't know any better, I would have thought that she was pregnant but she was supposed to be on birth control. After I made her lay down, I ran out to Walmart to grab a few pregnancy tests. When I got back home, she was still sleeping. I cleaned up the kitchen then took a shower. When I got out, Goddess was sitting on the edge of the bed looking like she was crying again.

"Goddess, what's wrong? Did something happen?"

"I don't know. I just woke up crying. I must have had a nightmare or something." I just looked at her because her ass was acting weird as fuck. Goddess got up to use the bathroom, but I stopped her.

"Hold on for a second before you use the bathroom," I told her while I went to get the pregnancy test. She looked at me funny but didn't say anything. I walked back in the room and handed her the test and she looked at me like I had three heads.

"Princeton, why the hell are you giving me a damn pregnancy test?"

"Because you're acting weird and you could be pregnant. Just take the test so we'll know."

"Fine. I'll take the fucking test but I know I'm not pregnant. Did you forget I was on birth control?" she snapped. Yeah, she had to be pregnant or done lost her damn mind talking to me like that. I didn't even say shit back. I just let her be. I dried off then put on some boxers, got into bed, and waited for her to come out. I swear it seemed like she was in there forever.

"Goddess, is everything okay?" I yelled. I heard sniffles then the bathroom door opened and her cheeks were wet. "What the hell are you crying for now?"

"Oh, God! I don't know how this happened. I'm pregnant, Princeton. I'm fucking pregnant!" Goddess cried falling into my arms. I ran my hands down my face trying to take in the news my damn self. This was a lot. Don't get me wrong, I wanted kids with her. A few if I could, but I really wanted a year or two just to enjoy my wife.

"It's okay, baby. Stop crying. Everything is gonna be okay. I got you and you know that. But at least we know why you been so damn weird and emotional. I thought you were on the depo?"

"I am. I'll make an appointment tomorrow to make sure." Nothing else was said. I just kissed her lips that led into a love making session. After sexing one another we both fell asleep.

Bang! Bang! Bang!

The sound of someone pounding on my door caused both of us to jump up from our sleep. I looked over at the clock and it was 3 a.m. I jumped up with my gun in my hand and snatched the door open to find Journey and Latrice at my door crying.

"Oh my God, what's wrong?" Goddess asked in a panicked tone.

"It's daddy! He was in car accident and their saying it's not looking too good," Journey cried. Goddess let out a scream that I would never forget. We both threw on some clothes and headed to Cooper's Hospital.

Goddess

When we got to the hospital, I barely let the car stop before I jumped out and headed to through the emergency doors.

"I'm her to see Rashaad Jenkins," I cried.

"May I ask your relationship to him?" the lady at the front desk asked, but I wasn't in the mood to answer a bunch of damn questions.

"I'm his fucking daughter that's who I am, but what fucking difference does it make? If we were called that means we're pretty damn important. Now, what room is my dad in?" I snapped. She looked like she wanted to say something smart, but I guess she saw our faces and decided not to which was a smart choice for her.

"He's currently in surgery. I'll let the doctor know that his family is here." I didn't say anything else. I just went and sat down next to my aunt Diana who was also crying. We hugged one another tightly.

"They're saying it was a pretty bad accident. It was even on the news. They said a drunk driver ran the red light and crashed into your dad's car and he flipped over," my aunt Diana told us. For some reason, it felt like my heart had stopped and I felt like I was gonna pass out. I couldn't stop the tears from falling because the thought of my father not making it caused my heart to stop. I was crying like a baby as Princeton rocked me back and forth in his arms. I was so out of it I wasn't even sure how I ended up in is arms.

"The family of Rashaad Jenkins?" the doctor came out and said. We all jumped up and rushed over to him so we could hear what he had to say.

"Rashaad is currently in a coma. We had to perform emergency surgery on him to drain the blood from his brain. It's not looking too good right now, but anything is possible. I have to be honest with you, I haven't seen many patients that survived something this severe and even if they did, they had little to no life in them," the doctor stated. At that very moment, I felt my chest tighten up and then stop and everything went black. When I opened my eyes, I panicked when I saw that I was hooked up to machines and I was confused because the last thing I remembered was coming here to see about my dad. How the hell I ended up in the hospital bed beats me. Princeton was right there by my side when I jumped up.

"What happened? Why am I here? Where's my dad!" I cried.

"Baby, you really need to calm down. You passed out is what happened. I know it's a lot to take in but you have to stay strong for the baby. I got you just relax," Princeton comforted me.

"Baby? Goddess, you're pregnant?" Journey quizzed.

"Yes. We found out a little after y'all left earlier so I need her to keep it together," Princeton answered for me.

"Damn, well congrats, big sis," Journey said sadly. Something else was going on with my sister I could tell.

"Where's daddy?" I asked getting straight to the point.

"He's still in a coma," she answered sadly.

"Daddy can't die. I would never be able to live without him. Who did this to him?" I cried. I wasn't sure how far along I was, but I hoped like hell that I wasn't gonna cry this entire pregnancy because that crying shit was annoying. All I could think about was my dad and what he meant to me. There was no way in hell that I could live without my dad. He was strong and I knew that he was gonna make it. I didn't care what those doctors were saying. "Did anyone call his girlfriend?" I asked.

"She knows because she was in the car with him. She's pretty fucked up too but she's just not as bad as daddy. We just came from her room."

The doctor walked in and asked was it okay to speak freely around everyone. I nodded yes since it was just my fiancé and sister in the room.

"The babies seem to be doing well. You look to be a little over eight weeks." The room got quiet and I had a confused look on my face.

"I'm sorry doctor but did you say babies as in more than one baby?" I asked, knowing I must have heard him incorrect.

"Yes, you're pregnant with twins and they seem to be in the same sack which means they're identical."

My eyes damn near popped out of my head. I wasn't even quite ready for one baby let alone two of them. "It is imperative that you take it easy. Pregnancy can already be hard but whenever you're pregnant with more than one is considered high risk. I understand this is a difficult time but you have to relax. You're dehydrated and your blood pressure was a little high so we have to keep you overnight just for observations."

"I can't stay here. I have to be around when my daddy wakes up."

"I'm sorry but you really need to stay," he replied.

"Can I talk to you outside?" Princeton asked the doctor. The doctor followed Princeton out the room. I looked over at Journey and she was crying. I knew she was crying about our dad because that man was our everything.

"Journey, I can't handle this and I'm trying to be strong, but it's just too much," I cried.

She came closer and hugged me tight. "Goddess, I'm scared. We've never been without him. What if he dies? What if he never gets to meet all of his grand kids?" She cried harder. I looked at her funny because she said all of his grand kids and I was only carrying two. Unless she was just talking in general.

"Journey, is there something you want to tell me?" She just looked at me for a few moments before speaking.

"I'm pregnant, too, but I'm early. I just found out a few days ago, but I'm only a month and I only found out during a regular routine checkup."

"Oh wow! What are the odds that both of us are pregnant at the same damn time? Have you told Perry, yet?"

"No I haven't. I was trying to find the right time and now that he may have another woman pregnant, I don't think I'm gonna tell him. I'm not even sure if I'm gonna keep the baby because I refuse to be a single mom."

"Journey I can't believe you're talking about getting an abortion! Daddy would kill you. But either way, Perry still has a right to know."

"I have a right to know what?" Perry asked walking through the door. The room fell silent and Journey looked at me with pleading eyes. Although I felt like she needed to tell him, it wasn't my place so I would let her tell him whenever she felt she was ready.

"Perry, why are you here?" Journey asked.

"What the fuck you mean why am I here? My girl father and sister are both laid up in the hospital and you really have the nerve to ask that? I know you upset with a nigga right now, but I'm always gonna be here for you no matter what. And I'm not going anywhere. Now, what exactly is it that I should know?" he asked again. Before she could say anything, Princeton walked back in the room.

"It cost me a pretty penny but they gonna put you in the room with your dad in the new rooms they have, so they about to move both of y'all in a minute. But Goddess, I need you to understand, he don't look good and I'm worried being in the room with him is gonna make you worse, so if you don't think you can handle it keep your ass in here. You heard what he doctor said. You have to take it easy when carrying twins."

"Twins? What the fuck am I missing?" Perry asked confused. The look on his face caused all three of us to laugh and that was just what I needed.

"Yeah, bro. Shit is crazy right now. We just find out a few minutes ago that we about to have identical twins."

"Damn. Well, congrats. You must be early as hell because you don't even look pregnant. Journey, don't think I forgot what you and Goddess was talking about. What is it that I should know?" Perry asked not letting up. Journey just shook her head and a single tear rolled down her face.

"I'm pregnant," she mumbled.

"Did you just say you're pregnant?" Perry asked.

She just nodded her head.

"Fuck," Perry mumbled and ran his hands down his face. "Let me talk to you alone," he said to Journey. She got up and followed him out. Two nurses came and took my vitals before they moved me in the room with my dad.

When we got up to the room my insides were doing back flips. I wasn't sure if I was ready to see my dad like that. Once I got in the room, I looked over at my dad and damn near passed out at the sight of him. He was hooked up to a million machines, his face looked two times bigger than normal, and there was a cast on his arm. I didn't make a scene, but I was crying a river. And my heart felt like it was about to pop out of my chest.

"Is there any way you can give her something to relax? This has been a long and trying day," Princeton asked the nurse.

"Yeah, just let me go get the doctor."

I decided that I needed to be alone with my dad just for a moment.

"I'm not trying to be rude, but I need a moment to be alone with my dad, please." Princeton looked like he was about to give me a hard time about it, but I gave him a look that let him know I wasn't for his shit at the moment. He just walked out the room and the nurse did the same. I walked over to my dad's bed and grabbed his hand that wasn't in a cast. The tears stained my cheeks as I talked to him.

"Daddy, please don't die on me. I can't live without you and I need you now more than ever before. Looking at you here in this bed like this is crushing my soul. Plus, you can't die right now. Who's gonna walk me down the aisle and give me away? Who's gonna help me with these two babies that I'm carrying? I don't know the first thing about being a mother. I know you're strong, you got this daddy. Please wake up. Don't do this to me and Journey. And daddy, you would never believe that Journey is also pregnant. Isn't it crazy how we both got pregnant at the same time? We already don't have a mom so we can't lose you, too," I cried. "I know you'll die one day but today is not the day," I cried loudly. I was no longer talking just crying a river. I guess I was so caught up with crying I didn't even realize that I had a room full of people until Journey wrapped her arms around me and hugged me tight as we cried over the possibility of our father dying.

The doctor came in and advised me to lie down so they could hook up the baby machine and give me something through my IV that would help me relax. I didn't even bother to argue because I was exhausted beyond words. After they checked me out and hooked me up to the machine, my ass was out like light.

One month later

Princeton and I just pulled up to Carrabba's in Cherry Hill for lunch. Today was my first official doctor's appointment that seemed to take forever but everything went great. The doctor said the babies were fine and I was now three months pregnant. We were able to hear the heart beats and they were strong as ever. I don't have to tell you that I cried and so did Princeton. We had our first ultrasound picture and the babies were so tiny they looked like little peanuts.

"Baby, you okay?" I asked Princeton. He looked a little spaced out.

"Yeah, I'm great babe. I'm actually happy. I can't wait to make you Mrs. Hughes," he answered.

"I can't wait to become Mrs. Hughes," I told him as I leaned forward to kiss his lips. Princeton was the best thing that has ever happened to me and he had proven to me time and time again that he was worthy of being my husband. Just in this past month alone he's been patient, caring, and understanding. All while trying to get his business off the ground, dealing with me, helping me get through the stuff with my father, and not to mention my pregnant hormonal ass. I was so grouchy at times but he knew how to put me in my place and still be passionate with me.

As soon as we left the restaurant, we headed to the hospital to see my dad. It was a month later and he was still in a coma. I still had faith that he would pull through for us while everyone was slowly but surely giving up. I went up there every day to talk to him. I haven't missed a day yet. Once his girlfriend Shantae made a full recovery, she was there just as much as I was. I could tell that she really loves my dad. When I walked in the room, I noticed that his head swelling looked back to normal and they had removed the cast from his arm. I stood at his bedside as I normally do with Princeton right by my side. I was sad that I would more than likely be postponing my wedding until my dad woke up from his coma because I wasn't walking down the aisle without him. Journey, Perry, and Ms. Shantae walked in right behind me. We haven't all been here together and at the same time since when it first happened.

"Hey daddy, it's Goddess. I'm not gonna stay long today, because your grandbabies are wearing me out already and they not even here yet. But I came to tell you that I'm now four months. I'm still not really showing. I just have a little baby bump. Daddy, I'm not giving up on you. I know you wouldn't leave me and Journey right now when we need you the most. But we do miss you and we just wanna hear your voice and look into your eyes. I love you so much, daddy."

"I love you, too, Princess," I heard and I damn near fainted at the sound of my dad's voice. He slowly opened his eyes and looked around the room in a confused state. All I could do was cry. I kissed him and the machines started beeping crazily. I started to panic because I was sure what that meant. A few moments later, the nurses rushed in and looked shocked and started calling for the doctors.

"Oh my God, I can't believe he's awake," I heard one of the nurses say on their way out the room. The doctor came in and asked us to clear the room so they could check him out but there was no way in hell I was going anywhere so they told us to move to the other side of the room and keep the noise down. I cried and hugged Princeton and my sister tightly. Once the doctor told my dad what happened and talked to him, he told us we could have a minute alone but then they had to run some test.

"How long was I in a coma?"

"A little over a month," I replied.

"Goddess, where are you? I can't see you," he stated but his eyes were open. So I started to panic.

"Daddy, you can't see us?" Journey asked.

"No, it's really blurry," he responded. Princeton ran to get the doctor before making us all leave out the room. I called my aunt Diana and Latrice to let them know what was going on.

Three hours later, the doctor finally told us we could go back to see him. When walked into the room, his head turned towards the door and smiled. My heart was filled with so much joy.

"Daddy, I'm so glad that you're awake. They tried to tell us you weren't gonna make, but I knew you would dad," I sobbed.

"God damn Goddess, are you gonna cry this entire pregnancy because that shits annoying," he said. I couldn't believe he said that. I burst out laughing so hard that I thought I pissed myself. The three of us laughed so hard.

"Wait, how did you know that I was pregnant?"

"I heard everything that you've said to me. I just couldn't respond and wasn't sure why. You're having twins, right? And Journey, you're also pregnant or did you get rid it because you think Perry was cheating on you and you don't wanna be a single mom?" I threw my hands over my mouth not believing that he heard all of that.

"I'm still pregnant, daddy," she mumbled.

"Good because I wouldn't have been too happy with you."

"Daddy, I love you so much. Thanks for not dying," Journey cried.

"No, thank God for giving me a second chance. Now go get my woman."

CHAPTER 12

Rashaad

E very day for what seemed like forever I would hear my family talking and crying at my bedside asking me to wake up. I could hear them but didn't know why I couldn't see them. But every time I heard my daughters crying and telling me their secrets, I fought to get up but just couldn't. It was something about the calmness of Goddess' voice that caused me to fight harder for some reason. It was the first time she had talked to me without crying the entire time. When I first woke up, I was able to hear them but not see them, but as the hours went on, I started to get my eyesight back. My girls were beautiful and looked vibrant, but I guess pregnancy would do it to you. I've been home for almost a month now. They thought I was gonna stay in that hospital for some damn physical therapy, but I hired my own to come out to the house. The girls came by every day of the damn week. I was happy as hell to see my kids but I just completed my physical therapy and now I wanted to see if my magic stick still worked properly. Goddess and Journey had just pulled up and I met them outside.

"How's my favorite girls?"

"We're good," they answered in unison.

"That's good to hear but listen, I love y'all to death but Shantae should be pulling up any minute and your daddy needs some pussy. I have to make sure this magic stick still got some magic."

"Oh my God, daddy, you're so nasty," Goddess said while shaking her head.

"Aight daddy, we get the poin.t I guess we have been a little overbearing and not respecting your privacy. We just not used to you having a woman," Journey stated.

"Y'all good and get used to her being around because I'm about to pop the question soon. I just don't know when but y'all get your asses away from my door and stop cock blocking."

As soon as Shantae walked through the door, I picked her ass up and carried her to my bedroom. I wasn't in the mood to do no talking. I laid her sexy ass on the bed and stripped her from every piece of clothing she had on. Looking at her naked body caused me to brick up immediately. I dove headfirst to lick on her sweetness. I licked her love button nice and slow in a circular motion while fingering her wetness. She was dripping all over my hands and into my mouth.

"Oh Rashaad," she cried out.

"Cum in my mouth, baby," I told her as I speed up my licks just a little faster. On cue, her body obeyed my command and she squirted in my mouth. After drinking it all up, I climbed on top of Shantae and kissed her lips and she moaned at the taste of her own juices. That shit turned me all the way on. I slid into her extra slippery tunnel, nice and slow. I stroked in and out of her at a slow pace but when she stared rocking her hips from the bottom, I sped up my strokes.

"Fuck, this pussy is good. You bet not ever give my pussy away, you hear me?"

"Yes Rashaad, I hear you. Ahh! Ahh! Oh God, I'm about to cum, Rashaad!"

"Then fucking cum. Don't tell, show me, wet this dick up. Come on, baby. Cream on my dick, baby," I groaned. I swear I wasn't ready to cum yet but the way that pussy was feeling, I knew I was about to bust. I watched Shantae cream all over my dick as I slid in and out of her. Her body started to seize and her mouth was hung open wide as she came all over my dick.

"Ahh shit, I'm cuming in this pussy," I yelled like a little bitch as I nutted hard.

After I rolled over and laid next to Shantae, I thought about our relationship. How much joy she brought into my life and I was ready to give her my last name and give my girls a stepmother. After we showered, I buzzed my cook and told her to make us something special and told her this was goanna be a very special night. I went out to my car to retrieve the ring I bought last week. Two hours later, everything was set up for two with rose petals, light music, and candles and of course, wine. After dinner was over, we sat, talked, and laughed. When the song "If This World Were Mine" came on, I knew this was the perfect time to ask.

"May I have this dance?" I asked standing up from my seat holding my hand out for hers. Shantae placed her hand in mine and I walked her to the dance floor. We slowed danced to the while gazing into one another eyes while singing the lyrics to the song.

"I love you so much Rashaad. I was scared to death when you were in that coma. I thought I had lost you," she said as a single tear fell from her face that I quickly kissed away.

"I love you, too, Shantae. How much do you love me?" I asked.

"I love you a lot Rashaad. My life would never be the same without you."

"So, do you love me enough to marry me and be wife?" I asked, dropping down on one knee. Shantae mouth fell open wide in shock. She covered her mouth but still didn't say anything. "An answer would be nice. These knees aren't what they use to be," I playfully said.

"OMG! God, yes Rashaad! I'll marry you," Shantae answered. I placed the ring on her finger and got from my knees while kissing her lips. I picked up my soon-to-be wife and carried her back into the bedroom and made love to her all night long then half of the morning.

Goddess

One year later

Life was good with my husband and twin daughters, Royalty and Majesty Hughes. I've never been so happy and complete in my life. Princeton was an even greater father than he was a husband and that was hard to top but he loved our twins more than life itself. At first, we had a hard time dealing with the fact that the girls were born at eight months and had to stay in the hospital for a few weeks but we finally adjusted to minor setbacks and stayed positive. Princeton's mom was now living in Jersey with us about two blocks away. Princeton brought us a big ass house after we got married in Deptford, New Jersey. His casinos were doing good and bringing in a shit load of money. I took a break from work just to focus on my kids. Not having a mother caused me to be extra clingy to my own. I never wanted them to feel like I did when I was growing up and even though my daddy did an excellent job with us, I still wanted a mom in my life. So, I vowed to be the be the best mother I could be. I'll never put anything or anyone in front of them. We had plenty of help with twins because even though they were a blessing, having twins wasn't easy. But with the help of his mom and dad, who got back together by the way, things are going great. Journey and Perry had a son and named him Javier. Journey wasn't playing when she said she wouldn't be with him until she found out if that baby was his or not and thank God it wasn't. They just got back together about a month ago and so far, they were doing pretty good. We all lived blocks away from one another all but my dad.

Although my daddy did move out of the house he was in, he lived about twenty-five minutes away from us. Him and my stepmom were still in the honeymoon stages and wanted their alone time. My dad told us that he did his job to the fullest and now it was time to let our husbands take care of us and I couldn't agree more. My dad felt like Journey was being stubborn when it came to Perry and that's why she wasn't married yet. My sister could definitely be stubborn but hey, we all were in our own little way. My dad sold a few of his night clubs so he now only had three and three cafés that all seemed to be doing well. I couldn't help but to admire my father and all that he is. If it wasn't for him, I don't know where I'll be. Married or not, I'll never love another man the way I love my dad. The fact that my father was once in the streets to take care of us but was able to get out and make an honest living is the exact reason I'm infatuated by a Street Legend and that Street Legend is my father Rashaad Jenkins.

The end
I really hoped you enjoyed this standalone
Infatuated by A Street Legend

CPSIA information can be obtained
at www.ICGtesting.com
Printed in the USA
LVHW111516011119
636084LV00002B/231/P

9 781697 004380